**"WHY ARE YOU HERE?"
SHE DEMANDED.**

"Because I love you," he said quietly. "And I'm not giving you up."

She laughed. "You're not? What about me? Oh, I forgot I have such poor judgment, according to you."

"Damn it, Kate," he exploded. "When I left, I thought I was giving myself time to think—and giving you time to think as well. It wasn't the end, not then. What happened? Why the letter?"

"You didn't even see the problem, Ben. You didn't even see that it was impossible, that it had to be over at some point. Don't you see? There's no chance for us. You've never seen that you're constantly driving me away." She sighed, her eyes filling with tears. "Maybe that's why I fell in love with you, because I knew you really didn't want me. You were like all the others—safe, unattainable, predictable. But I'm different now. I want a man who really, truly loves me. And that's not you."

A CANDLELIGHT ECSTASY ROMANCE ®

138 WHITE SAND, WILD SEA, *Diana Blayne*
139 RIVER ENCHANTMENT, *Emma Bennett*
140 PORTRAIT OF MY LOVE, *Emily Elliott*
141 LOVING EXILE, *Eleanor Woods*
142 KINDLE THE FIRES, *Tate McKenna*
143 PASSIONATE APPEAL, *Elise Randolph*
144 SURRENDER TO THE NIGHT, *Shirley Hart*
145 CACTUS ROSE, *Margaret Dobson*
146 PASSION AND ILLUSION, *Bonnie Drake*
147 LOVE'S UNVEILING, *Samantha Scott*
148 MOONLIGHT RAPTURE, *Prudence Martin*
149 WITH EVERY LOVING TOUCH, *Nell Kincaid*
150 ONE OF A KIND, *Jo Calloway*
151 PRIME TIME, *Rachel Ryan*
152 AUTUMN FIRES, *Jackie Black*
153 ON WINGS OF MAGIC, *Kay Hooper*
154 A SEASON FOR LOVE, *Heather Graham*
155 LOVING ADVERSARIES, *Eileen Bryan*
156 KISS THE TEARS AWAY, *Anna Hudson*
157 WILDFIRE, *Cathie Linz*
158 DESIRE AND CONQUER, *Diane Dunaway*
159 A FLIGHT OF SPLENDOR, *Joellyn Carroll*
160 FOOL'S PARADISE, *Linda Vail*
161 A DANGEROUS HAVEN, *Shirley Hart*
162 VIDEO VIXEN, *Elaine Raco Chase*
163 BRIAN'S CAPTIVE, *Alexis Hill Jordan*
164 ILLUSIVE LOVER, *Jo Calloway*
165 A PASSIONATE VENTURE, *Julia Howard*
166 NO PROMISE GIVEN, *Donna Kimel Vitek*
167 BENEATH THE WILLOW TREE, *Emma Bennett*
168 CHAMPAGNE FLIGHT, *Prudence Martin*
169 INTERLUDE OF LOVE, *Beverly Sommers*
170 PROMISES IN THE NIGHT, *Jackie Black*
171 HOLD LOVE TIGHTLY, *Megan Lane*
172 ENDURING LOVE, *Tate McKenna*
173 RESTLESS WIND, *Margaret Dobson*
174 TEMPESTUOUS CHALLENGE, *Eleanor Woods*
175 TENDER TORMENT, *Harper McBride*
176 PASSIONATE DECEIVER, *Barbara Andrews*
177 QUIET WALKS THE TIGER, *Heather Graham*

TURN BACK THE DAWN

Nell Kincaid

A CANDLELIGHT ECSTASY ROMANCE ®

Published by
Dell Publishing Co., Inc.
1 Dag Hammarskjold Plaza
New York, New York 10017

ISBN: 0-440-19098-3

Printed in the United States of America
First printing—October 1983

To Our Readers:

We have been delighted with your enthusiastic response to Candlelight Ecstasy Romances®, and we thank you for the interest you have shown in this exciting series.

In the upcoming months we will continue to present the distinctive sensuous love stories you have come to expect only from Ecstasy. We look forward to bringing you many more books from your favorite authors and also the very finest work from new authors of contemporary romantic fiction.

As always, we are striving to present the unique, absorbing love stories that you enjoy most—books that are more than ordinary romance.

Your suggestions and comments are always welcome. Please write to us at the address below.

Sincerely,

The Editors
Candlelight Romances
1 Dag Hammarskjold Plaza
New York, New York 10017

CHAPTER ONE

Up on the eighth floor of Ivorsen and Shaw, a large specialty store on East Fifty-second Street, Kate Churchill picked up the phone and pushed the flashing "intercom" button. "Yes, Linda?"

"The people from Blake-Canfield Advertising are here, Kate."

"Thanks. Ask them to wait, please, and I'll be with them in a few minutes."

"Right," Linda said, and hung up.

Kate replaced the receiver and swiveled her chair around to face Kurt Reeves, who was standing behind her and looking out the window.

"So your guests are here," he said sulkily, his back still turned. "And your little secret from the art department has to leave."

Kate sighed. "Kurt, please. Don't start."

He turned to face her, looking even more boyish than his twenty-six years. He was blond with the good looks of a surfer, and Kate liked him, but she was beginning to tire of his childish moods. More important, she was beginning to tire of his games, not the least of which was his probable infidelity. She wasn't certain of it; she had heard the rumor only yesterday, when her best friend had told her that Kurt might be seeing another woman. And she hadn't yet said anything to him of her suspicions. For she knew it was time, other woman or not, to end it. And perhaps ending it simply, with no recriminations, would be best.

"Are you free tonight?" he asked, in a voice that suggested he half-hoped she wasn't.

"I don't know," she said. She hesitated, loath to say more. "We'll talk later, okay? I have people waiting out there to see me."

His eyes sparked with interest. "Which ones are these? Gallagher Media?"

"No, they were yesterday. Today is Blake-Canfield. They've done the ads for that new diet soda and for National Express."

"I'm impressed. Why don't I stay for the meeting?" Kurt asked, trying to charm her with his smile.

Kate shook her head. "Sorry. If I choose them, you'll meet them later on."

"Kate, I *am* acting art director. I don't see why I haven't been in on all the meetings."

She sighed, running her hands through her thick black hair. The heat in the building was on even though it was only October, and she was warm even in her short-sleeved silk blouse and skirt. "Kurt, come on. That's just the way it is."

She had hardly given a thought to her words, had said them almost automatically. But when she looked up at Kurt, he was smarting, looking at her with a resentment that was shocking in its intensity. "You're perfectly happy to go out with me, Kate. When it's a secret. But you know, you treat me like dirt in the office. It's only outside that we have any kind of decent relationship."

"I'm not so sure about that," she said.

He blinked. "What's that supposed to mean?"

She sighed. She hadn't intended to get into a serious discussion—not now, right before a meeting.

"What about tonight?" he suddenly demanded.

"I don't know," she said. "We'll talk later."

He gave her a look of annoyance. "All right," he said in a vaguely threatening voice. "I might give you a call." And he left, slamming the door behind him.

She sighed. Sometimes she didn't know what she had ever seen in him. He was extremely attractive, of course, but she knew she wouldn't have begun seeing him if there hadn't been more to him than just his looks. Yet the relationship was definitely over now. He was so young, and though she had always—since college, anyway—tended to involve herself with men who, in the end, wanted only a superficial relationship, Kurt was trying even her limits. For although he was often petulant, even whiny, at work, he was dominating in every other respect, taking out his resentments on Kate in a thousand different ways.

Her predilection for men who were distant emotionally or in other ways was a form of self-protection she had developed early on, and though it always led her into frustrating, no-win situations, she found herself unable to change. Whenever there was a man who seemed "wrong"—whether because he was too wild or too good looking or too inaccessible—she was attracted to him as powerfully as if he were the most perfect man in the world. And naturally, because he was "wrong" in some way, the relationship would inevitably end sooner than Kate wanted it to; and it often ended very unpleasantly as well.

Kate had often tried to analyze why she was so unsuccessful in this area of her life while in most others she had done so well. But she was too close to the problem to be able to see its causes. She knew that she hadn't had a particularly good example of relationships when she was growing up: her father had left their home in New York City when Kate was five, and her mother had since been married twice and gone out with a series of inappropriate, often married, men. But Kate knew that could hardly be the only reason for her behavior.

And she didn't, in fact, even think her skepticism about relationships was all that misguided. After all, with so many marriages crumbling into divorce these days, what was the point of making marriage a serious goal? She certainly wasn't going to fall into that trap. She wouldn't close herself off completely from the idea, of course; if she met the right man, and if she wanted to, and if *he* wanted to, they would get married. But it sounded like an awful lot of if's to her.

In the meantime she had other more important things to worry about, one of them being the new ad campaign designed to put Ivorsen and Shaw back on the map. The store's once-glowing image had tarnished over the past fifteen years, growing old along with its customers. Once the city's leading specialty store, it now had almost no image: private-school kids thought of it as the kind of place they would be forced to go to for school clothes if they didn't fight for Bloomingdale's instead; mothers thought of it as proper but perhaps a bit staid and certainly too expensive; and old women loved it, but didn't have the money to do much more than walk through the store and stop for lunch at the restaurant on the seventh floor.

But the store was in the last stages of a major renovation and redesign, and Kate had great hopes for its future. With its new look and the new campaign it had a good chance of recapturing its former place in the city's pantheon of luxury stores.

Kate felt as strongly about Ivorsen and Shaw as if the store were her own. In a sense she felt it was. She had grown up with the store, learning all she knew about her field in her rise from secretary to director of advertising and promotion. Now she would have a chance to give back some of what the store had given her; she would put into practice all the ideas, tricks, and plans that could help put Ivorsen and Shaw back in the spotlight. The store's revenues were the lowest they had been in years, and if Kate didn't help turn the situation around, she would be out of her job as quickly as her predecessor; he had lasted exactly six months.

Kate stood up and glanced in the mirror on the wall. She had been working hard, and it showed; her dark brown eyes had dark gray circles underneath, and her pale skin looked almost translucent. But her hair—straight, jet-black, shoulder-length with wisps of bangs—looked good. And with the new clothes she was wearing—a short-sleeved lavender silk blouse and skirt—she knew she looked presentable.

She turned and walked back to her desk and asked Linda to send the people from Blake-Canfield in, then walked across the soft carpeting to the door so she could greet her guests as they came in.

The first—young, red-haired, looking no more than a

boy—introduced himself as Tommy Sullivan, assistant art director. He looked a bit wild-eyed and cocky, as if he were keeping a very pleasant secret, and Kate wondered whether his excitement was over the layouts he had under his arm. She certainly hoped so—she had great expectations for Blake-Canfield's presentation. And if Blake-Canfield's work didn't look promising, there was only one agency to go to before starting the bids all over again.

But Kate's worries and speculations disappeared as she took the hand of the man who stepped in after Tommy Sullivan.

He took her hand warmly and firmly in his, and when she looked into his hazel eyes, she thought they were the warmest, most compelling eyes she had ever seen. "I'm Ben Austin," he said, in a rich, warm voice that fit his handshake and his eyes. "It's nice to meet you and connect a real person to the voice I've spoken to on the phone."

She smiled. "Yes. Finally. Well, please sit down." She looked at Ben Austin as he walked to the far end of the oval-shaped conference table. He definitely fit the voice she had liked so much over the past few weeks. He looked to be in his early forties, with the same surprisingly easy manner she had noticed in her conversations with him. There was nothing studied about the man: from the dark, gray-templed hair that went straight back in no particular style, to his clothes, he looked like a man who did what he wanted as he wanted. He was dressed much more casually than other account executives she had met recently, in a brown Harris tweed jacket, a heathery-hued plaid shirt, and black corduroy pants. And, aside from his attractiveness, there was something relaxing in the approach: with other account executives Kate always felt as if they desperately wanted something from her—which, naturally, they did. But the feeling that she was their last dying hope always made her uncomfortable and unreceptive. Ben Austin, on the other hand, looked as if he had all he wanted; and if he wanted something from you, you'd be only too glad to help.

He smiled at her gaze of appraisal. "We didn't get where we are by playing games, Miss Churchill—either of us. You were, I'm sure, expecting the usual presentation, with an account executive—yours truly—promising you the world and assuring you you'll be our most prized client. You and I both also know that the worst thing an agency can do is come in and give the impression it needs the account." He smiled—a winning, friendly smile. "Acting desperate has never helped get anyone hired." He paused, his eyes shining as he leaned back and pulled a pipe out of the pocket of his jacket. He raised a brow. "Mind?" he asked softly.

"Please go ahead," she said. She loved the smell of good pipe tobacco—rich, sweet, woodsy—and she instinctively knew that anything owned or used by Ben Austin would be the best there was.

Kate watched as he tamped the tobacco into his pipe. His hands were tan and strong-looking, and there was something easy and very appealing in the way he moved: he was obviously comfortable with his attractiveness, aware of it but not obsessed with it. Perhaps one reason for this, Kate speculated, was that he wasn't classically all that perfect-looking: his nose was slightly off-center and looked as if it had once been broken, and he had a somewhat weathered look, with smile lines at the sides of his eyes and mouth. But he was one of the most attractive men Kate had ever met.

When Ben began to speak again, Kate once again felt the appeal of his voice—low, rich, smooth. It took hold of her gently, brought her close, until she felt she was a breath away. "Generally," he observed, "the more you try to convince a person of something, the more he or she resists. After all"—he again raised his eyebrow—"there must be some reason you're using the hard sell." He smiled. "Needless to say, I hope I'm right in assuming we can break through all that nonsense. Quite simply, Miss Churchill, you know that every agency can use another account. With all the awards we've gotten this year, we're hardly hurting, but naturally we'd like to handle more. However." His eyes penetrated hers. "I don't consider this just another account. The revitalization of Ivorsen and Shaw is one of the most exciting concepts we've worked on since the formation of the agency—and one of the most challenging I've worked on in my entire career. For both of us, I think, this could be a very exciting campaign. One I don't want to miss." He paused, and as Kate was drawn into the depths of his hazel gaze, she felt as if she were alone in the room with Ben Austin, as if he were beckoning her to the warmth of his strong arms.

Suddenly, she was aware that she and Austin had been looking into each other's eyes for a long, long moment. And Tommy Sullivan was probably waiting for one of them to speak.

"Well," Austin said, as if he, too, had to pull himself up out of a haze. "As we see it, your store essentially has no market at the moment—no one group of buyers that can be broken down meaningfully in terms of age, economic status, or anything else. But after having spoken to Stewart Carey—your man who's organizing the new buying strategies—I think the problem is challenging but workable. Carey is gearing the entire store—from lingerie to the new one-of-a-kind furniture department—back to what it used to be known for—mid- to high-priced items, all of exceptional quality that you would find at few, if any, other stores in the area.

"The problem—as he sees it and as we see it—is that somewhere along the way, the image was lost. People just saw Ivorsen and Shaw as a dusty old expensive store with dusty old expensive things no one could really afford. The key, Miss Churchill, is that people have to know what to expect. No one walks out of Cartier and says, 'I had no idea the prices would be so high.' It's a luxury store, and you go when you want that sort of thing. And remember—you may not go into Cartier every day of the week to buy earrings for yourself, but when you have to give a dear friend something special, chances are you'd go there rather than to a discount store or even something in between. There's a place in many, many people's lives for a store like Ivorsen and Shaw. So. The plan is essentially one of image building, and saturation. And I think we've come up with something you'll like." He smiled, his warm hazel eyes smiling, too. "We'd like to establish the Ivorsen and Shaw couple—young, attractive, moving up in the world. In TV spots, radio spots, print ads, and in person, this young man and woman will buy, argue, plan, even wish for certain items they can't quite afford. And you'll have your image right there—something people can either accept or reject, but they'll know what they're getting."

Kate smiled. She liked the idea. And as Austin went on

with the concept and the campaign plans, she liked it more. Austin introduced Tommy Sullivan again and went through some sample magazine layouts they had put together, and then summarized the campaign once more. He finished up by saying they were prepared—obviously—to work up more ideas, but that what they had done so far was the campaign they would recommend over all others.

Kate smiled. "Well, thank you very much. I like it a lot—I must say that. But I have other agencies to see. So—I'll let you know by next Friday at the latest. Naturally I'll be meeting with some other store people, too. But in any case it will be next Friday that you'll know." She looked into Ben Austin's eyes. "And I must say it does look promising." The moment she saw his eyes shine with pleasure, she regretted her words. The decision, after all, wouldn't be entirely hers, and while it would have been pointless and silly to pretend to be neutral, she had just given them all the encouragement possible, short of actually saying yes. Now, if the Ivorsen and Shaw corporate brass decided they wanted to see other campaigns from Blake-Canfield, Kate would have to come back to the agency as someone whose judgment had obviously been overruled.

"I'm glad you're pleased," Austin said, interrupting her thoughts. "But I won't allow myself any real pleasure until I've heard from you again." His voice was like a caress, stroking her outside and in, and the way he had said "pleasure" as he looked into her eyes made her feel as if his real pleasure at that moment would be to brush his lips against hers.

"Yes, you don't want to be premature," she said vaguely, then snapped herself out of the prison his eyes were holding her in. "But as I said," she added crisply, "Friday at the latest."

Austin smiled. "I'll look forward to it." He turned to Tommy Sullivan. "I'd like a few words alone with Miss Churchill, Tommy." He looked at his watch. "And then I'm off to lunch. So I'll see you back at the office."

A spark of surprise flashed in Tommy Sullivan's eyes, and he stood up. "Sure," he said. "See you later." He gathered up his portfolio, said good-bye to Kate, then turned and said a quick good-bye to Austin.

After he had left, conspicuously shutting the door behind him, Kate looked questioningly at Austin. "What was that all about?" she asked. "Why did he look so upset?"

Ben shrugged. "You know agencies and how insecure a lot of people are. He was let go from his last place, and who knows? He might have thought I wanted to be alone with you so I could tell you we'd be bringing in another art person next week. Those stories about coming back from lunch and finding your desk in the mail room are true, you know."

Kate shook her head. "That's awful. Is it really so cutthroat at Blake-Canfield?"

"Well, yes and no. We're growing now, thank God, so the chances of layoffs are low at the moment. But I can understand a kid like that. His job means a lot to him, and the Ivorsen and Shaw campaign is his first one with Blake-Canfield, so naturally he's nervous."

Kate frowned. "That doesn't sound like a particularly pleasant atmosphere to work in. I don't think I would do very well knowing that my job was in constant jeopardy."

She paused, aware that he seemed to be only half-listening. His hazel gaze was taking in her eyes, her hair, her mouth, and while he was making her feel self-conscious, it was in a very pleasurable way. Clearly, he liked what he saw. "So," she said, smiling. "I'm sure you didn't stay on after the meeting to hear my feelings about office politics. What was it you wanted to talk about?"

He smiled. "Well. When you ask me flat out, I have no choice other than to answer flat out." His eyes sparkled. "I had planned to charm and lull you into such a state that you'd hardly give the question a thought."

"And what was the question?" she asked, smiling.

"Are you free for lunch?" he said softly. "Or dinner."

A wave of apprehension mixed with excitement swept through her. *He's making this too easy,* she thought. *Which means I'll be all the more trapped.* She was saved, though, from replying, by the buzzing of the intercom on her desk. She gave Ben a noncommittal glance and went over to the phone. "Yes, Linda."

"Kurt Reeves, Kate."

"Please tell him I'm in a meeting and I'll call him back."

"I did," Linda said. "But he insisted."

Kate sighed. "All right. I'll take it. Thanks." She pushed the flashing red button down and spoke. "Yes, Kurt."

"Hey," he said softly. "I just wanted to know about tonight—whether we were on or not."

She hesitated, acutely conscious that Ben Austin was in the room and probably listening. "I don't know," she said.

"Kate, it's been a long time."

That was too much. "At whose insistence, Kurt? I

thought you were the one who said things were getting too complicated."

"Yeah, well, maybe I was wrong."

She sighed and glanced over at Ben Austin. He was looking at his presentation, apparently not listening. But she still didn't feel comfortable. "Look, Kurt. I'm really not in a position to talk right now," she said, her voice almost a whisper. "And I don't even know what I want to say to you at this point anyway. I need some time to think."

"But Kate—"

"I'll talk to you later," she said, and hung up before he could say anything else.

As she started for the table, Austin closed the folder he had been looking through. "Sorry," he said, turning to look at her. "I should have offered to leave the room."

She shook her head. "No, that's all right," she said. "If I had wanted you to leave, I could have asked."

He looked at her carefully. "Something tells me we're not going to be sharing lunch or dinner."

She smiled. She was actually very tempted to take Austin up on his invitation—if out of spite rather than anything else. But she resisted. Her natural impulses tended to lead her—inevitably—in the wrong direction. And whatever reckless attraction and temptation she felt, she would be wise to suppress. "Not today," she said, compromising with herself.

"I know the conversation wasn't for me to overhear," he said softly, "but you do deserve better, you know."

She said nothing. Protest would have been natural—saying that he didn't know anything about Kurt or about her, that it was none of his business anyway. But somehow, when she looked into his dark-lashed amber eyes, she knew that he truly did think she deserved better. She half-smiled. "You may be right. But I try to make it a rule not to discuss one man with another. It doesn't seem fair."

He tilted his head. "As if men were members of another species, Kate? I don't see anything unfair about it." He smiled. "Anyway, I'm sure you don't give away any more than you want to."

"Perhaps," she said, thinking nothing could be farther from the truth. "But really—why don't we just drop it for the moment."

He pursed his lips and gazed at her thoughtfully. "Well. I can see when I've been beaten. But, Kate, I did want to get together with you before you made your decision."

She raised a brow. "Before?" She smiled. "So you can sway me in your favor?"

"Would that be possible?" he asked softly.

A slow smile began as she looked into his eyes. "I think so."

"Let's," he murmured.

For a moment, as his amber gaze held her eyes in a simmering pull of warmth, as she was aware of his nearness, his scent, his obvious desire, she thought he might lean over and kiss her. She almost hoped he would, yet feared it. For she knew she would melt under one touch of his warm hands, one breath against her cheek, one touch of his lips against hers.

She wanted to look away. The pull was too intense; there were too many unknowns.

But he was making her feel wonderful—desirable, beautiful, wanted. And she wanted to flirt, to watch him respond, to know that he wanted her.

And so, instead of looking away, or backing off, or pretending she didn't notice the heated wanting in his gaze, she kept her eyes on his. She slowly inhaled, her heart racing as the warmth in their gaze burst into flame. And then she reached out and gently stroked his hand.

The moment she touched him, he drew in his breath sharply, and she knew that for him, as for her, the touch was like fire. "Sometime," she said softly. "Whenever this is all over."

His eyes were heavy with desire, and his hand moved and covered hers, sending waves of warm need through her.

"Why not sooner?" he murmured. "Why not tonight?"

She smiled—a lazy, seductive smile that took all the edge off the words she next said. "You know very well. We've already agreed. There's the not very small matter of undue influence."

Looking into her eyes, he stroked the palm of her hand with a coaxing touch that made her breathless, made her think of all the ways he could make her tremble with pleasure. "I wish you didn't feel that way," he said quietly. "But I think I understand. I don't promise to play by your rules, Kate, but I promise I'll try."

A few minutes later, after Ben had left, Kate wondered whether she hadn't already been unduly influenced. For she couldn't forget the enticing beckoning of his hazel eyes, couldn't wait to feel his gentle touch and hear his caressing voice once again.

Later on, as her memory of Ben Austin had been colored by events of the day, she wondered: had he been all that she had thought—charming, sincere, attractive—or had she only made him seem that way? For as she looked forward to the bleak prospect of making a decision about Kurt, she knew that subconsciously, at least, Kurt's bad qualities were making Ben Austin look very good indeed.

And if she knew herself—which, at the age of thirty, she felt she did—she was interested in someone who was certain to turn out to be yet another Mr. Wrong.

CHAPTER TWO

The next day Kate saw the last of the presentations for the new ad campaign. While this agency had all the enthusiasm she could ask for, there was no question about the presentation; in terms of goals, strategies, and actual content, Blake-Canfield's had been far and away the most promising. Now all she had to do was convince Dick Dayton and Andrew Smithfield, the two Ivorsen and Shaw board members who had traditionally—for a total of at least fifty years, from what Kate could tell—ruled on advertising matters.

Later in the afternoon, as she assembled the presentations of the three agencies on the conference table, she wondered: was the difference between Blake-Canfield's and the other two as obvious as she felt it was? She had always been thoroughly professional in her work, trying not to allow her personal feelings to affect her judgment. With Kurt, for instance, she had always been completely straightforward about his work, even at the height of her involvement with him: if she thought something looked great, she told him, and if she thought something looked like hell, she told him that, too. But now, with Ben Austin's work, she wasn't altogether certain she was acting completely impartially.

For there was something eating away at her, grabbing at her heart even as she looked at the presentations. She wanted to see him again. She couldn't get around that thought, or pretend it didn't exist, or separate it from her feelings about his work. For even as she looked at something as prosaic as his sales projections, she imagined him coming around behind her, putting his arms around her waist, gently kissing the back of her neck. She imagined how he would feel standing behind her—his hard thighs against the softness of her shape, his strong arms clasping her gently yet firmly, the touch of his lips that would send shimmering waves of desire through her.

I'm losing my mind, she thought, and turned away from the presentations.

And a few moments later she was repeating those words to her closest and most level-headed friend, Alison Hammond.

"Listen, Ally, how about dinner tonight, my treat?"

"Sure. I'd love to. But why your treat? Oh, that's right, I forgot about that ill-deserved raise you got!"

Kate laughed. "Come on. I'm sure you'll be next. Your department hasn't even come up for review."

"Mm. Well. We shall see. So what's the problem? Kurt?"

"Oh, partly. I'll tell you later."

They made arrangements to meet at the Fifty-second Street entrance to the store at five thirty and hung up, and Kate went back to work feeling better able to concentrate. She would simply put Ben *and* Kurt out of her mind until dinner.

* * *

Later on, at the dark and noisy Mexican restaurant Alison and Kate always went to when they wanted to talk about office politics, men, and other matters best not overheard, Kate told Alison all about Ben.

"The worst thing about it," Kate said, scooping up a big mound of guacamole on a taco chip, "is that I have the feeling I'm doing it all over again. I just can't get him out of my mind." She sighed. "But that's exactly the way I felt with Kurt. And look at *that* relationship."

Alison frowned, her usually pretty face shadowed with tension. "Hey, listen. I heard something today I think you should know."

Kate looked up. "What is it?"

"It's about Kurt. It *is* definite, Kate. He was seeing Cynthia Williston. I don't know if it's still going on, but—"

Kate waved a hand. "Look. I feel horrible about it. But I realized it earlier today, when I was talking to him. It just all fell into place—the evasiveness, the fact that he didn't want to see me that much, but then at other times he was 'suddenly free.' Hell, he didn't even try to hide it. Since we work together, he could hardly say he had business meetings to go to." She sighed. "What I mind most is that it doesn't bother me—because I don't even like Kurt anymore, Ally. And that's what gets me. He isn't at all what I had thought he was. So I've done it again."

Alison shook her head. "Hey, listen. It isn't just you, Kate. If we could all predict how our relationships would come out, we wouldn't give the time of day to half the men we go out with." She took a sip of wine. "Look at me.

Divorced twice. Twice, and I'm thirty-two! At least you don't have that to think about."

"In a way I'd rather that were true of me. I haven't even gotten that close to commitment, because the men I choose always end up being so wrong for me. Nothing like marriage ever comes up."

Alison shrugged. "That may be, but you've got to look ahead and quit letting the past drag you down. It sounds corny, but it's true. And anyway, I don't see what's so wrong with this Ben Austin. From what you've told me, he sounds magnificent—smart, sincere, good-looking, secure, great job, obviously likes you, what else do you need? Hell, I'll take him if you're not interested."

Kate widened her eyes, and Alison laughed. "See, you really do want him. Maybe you're a little apprehensive because you think he might be *right,* Kate—not because you think he's another Mr. Wrong."

Kate smiled. "Come on. That just couldn't be true."

"We'll see about that. And listen—I know we both pig out when we're preoccupied, but if you eat one more of those tacos I'm going to break your legs. Get your mind *off* this Ben Austin, *off* these tacos, and on to something else, okay?"

Kate laughed, and for the rest of the evening she tried to relax and have a good time. But she couldn't shake her doubts. Ben *had* seemed wonderful; he *had* seemed sincere. But as she looked back on it now, the whole encounter seemed too smooth. It was easy for a man like Ben to overhear an obviously strained conversation between a man and a woman and say, "I understand." It was easy for him to look at her with gentle amber eyes and tell her without words that he understood. But it could all have been an act, one to which she was especially vulnerable at the moment. And he had been noticeably close-mouthed about his own life. What did she even know about him?

And so, though she didn't voice her feelings to her friend—she just couldn't face another pep talk at the moment—she decided that, if nothing else, she would be damned careful around Ben Austin. There would have to be a lot more than desire in those golden eyes of his for her to be interested in him.

The next morning Kate's only thoughts of Ben Austin concerned the campaign he had developed. In all of her musings of the evening before, she had completely lost sight of the fact that she had a difficult task ahead of her: convincing Dick Dayton and Andrew Smithfield that her choice of Blake-Canfield was the best one. For while there was now no doubt in her mind that she was correct, she was realistic enough to know that Dayton and Smithfield wouldn't necessarily agree with her. They were both as conservative as could be, refusing to face the fact that Ivorsen and Shaw would have to develop a new image if it were going to recapture even a fraction of its former market. And Blake-Canfield's campaign—with its emphasis on youth and fashion—was anything but conservative.

But she was confident nevertheless. She hadn't gotten to be director of advertising and promotion by being weak, and she had faced more difficult challenges in the past.

An hour after lunch, however, as she sat once more at the head of the table, with Dick Dayton to her left and Andrew Smithfield to her right, she felt her confidence rush away with the swiftness of an ocean tide as Mr. Smithfield said, not to her but to his colleague across the table, "Well, Dick, it seems obvious to me that the Blake-Canfield plan is the least workable of the three."

Kate couldn't believe it. She had just finished her opening statement; she had just given five reasons why the Blake-Canfield campaign was her choice; she couldn't possibly have made her position any clearer. And Andrew Smithfield had spoken not only as if he hadn't heard her, but as if she weren't even there.

Dick Dayton frowned and shook his head. "Couldn't agree with you more." He picked up the sheaf of papers that represented the Blake-Canfield campaign and held them away to read at a distance. Kate knew he was farsighted, and needed to hold the papers that way; yet the gesture, with Dayton's perpetual slight grimace, looked like one of mild distaste, and Kate was incensed.

"Gentlemen," she said, holding her voice in check, "perhaps it would help if you explained exactly what you find unworkable. Then I can respond to specific questions and points."

Dick Dayton grimaced some more and then nodded at Andrew Smithfield. "Drew, it's the old problem, isn't it?"

Smithfield shrugged as if there were no question about its being "the old problem"—whatever that was. "Of course," Smithfield said. Finally, he looked at Kate. "You see, Miss Churchill, over the years we've had advertising directors come and advertising directors go." There was a glimmer of a smile as he spoke, but then it disappeared. "And over the years, young men—and young women like yourself—have from time to time suggested campaigns along the line of Blake-Canfield's proposed campaign." He smiled and narrowed his eyes. "Almost a matter of reinventing the wheel, you might say. And in each case,

Miss Churchill, we've had to suggest other courses of action. An Ivorsen and Shaw spokesman—whether a man or a woman or both—simply isn't practical, workable, or feasible."

Kate looked at him without emotion. "You used the word 'unworkable' before, Mr. Smithfield, but aside from using the word, you haven't let me know why."

Smithfield glanced at Dayton as if they were both in the presence of a less-than-intelligent outsider. He sighed, steepled his fingers, and looked back at Kate. "Troubles. Pure and simple, Miss Churchill. This young man and woman you propose: they'll be actors, will they not? And when he gets summoned to Hollywood and she gets her pretty little self pregnant, what then?"

"Oh. You're right," she said. "Of course. But if you're going to worry about maternity leave, why not paternity? And while we're worrying, what about illness, war, floods, famine, all those things that can cut so drastically into one's production schedule?" She sighed. "Mr. Smithfield, I don't mean to be sarcastic, but really—I don't understand what you're worried about. Plays and movies and TV series and commercials are shot all the time. Some go over schedule and over budget, others don't. Some actors and actresses drop out or are fired for one reason or another, others are fine. But surely—if that's your only objection, I think you might reexamine it in light of other projects in many different kinds of media. Remember—we're talking about the survival of Ivorsen and Shaw—not some abstract plan. And nothing that any of the previous directors ever instituted came close to turning the red ink black."

Neither one of the men was pleased with her response.

Perhaps, she felt, they had expected immediate acquiescence in the face of their objections; she neither knew nor cared. For the next forty minutes, though, she answered each one of their objections. And finally they gave in, when she pointed out the deficiencies of the other presentations and the fact that they would have to start the agency search all over again if they didn't agree on Blake-Canfield. With their agreement came the very clear implication that if the campaign didn't produce the excellent results Kate had forecast, she would go out with the campaign. But she wasn't going to worry about that now. Now, she would concentrate on making the campaign work as well as she possibly could, without thought of failure. Because, despite the skepticism shown by Dayton and Smithfield, the Blake-Canfield campaign was the best anyone could have come up with.

A few moments after Dayton and Smithfield left, Kate dialed Ben's office. Though she had imagined at least a half a dozen times making the call, she hadn't known how jumpy she'd feel. Now that her adversaries were gone and she had won, it was as if she was finally allowing herself to feel all the tension that had been there during the meeting. Her adrenaline was flowing, her heart was pounding, and the moment she heard the words "Blake-Canfield Advertising," her knees were like jelly.

She had won. And now there was no turning back. Whether Ben was Mr. Right or Mr. Wrong or destined to be merely a friend, Ben Austin was going to be part of her life over the coming weeks. And suddenly she was uncomfortably nervous.

"Ben Austin," came his voice, interrupting her thoughts with that low caress that made her tremble.

"Hi. It's Kate Churchill."

There was a silence. Then: "Tell me you have good news, Kate."

She smiled and sank into her chair. "I do," she said.

"Fantastic. That is the best news I've had in I don't know how long!" he cried. "That's wonderful. So. Next step next. To get together. How does your schedule look tomorrow? How about meeting from ten or so on through lunch? This is wonderful, you know—getting a jump on the schedule like this. So how about it?"

She smiled. It was the first time she had ever heard him sound "Madison Avenue," talking a mile a minute. "Well, let's see," she said, looking at her calendar and crossing off "facial at Georgette Klinger" scheduled for twelve o'clock. "Sure, Ben—that'll work out."

"Wonderful." He paused for a moment. "And really, Kate, I can't tell you how much I'm looking forward to working with you."

"Yes, well, I feel the same way," she said vaguely, her mind not at all on what she was saying. For hearing the slight huskiness of his voice, remembering the dark-lashed amber of his eyes and the warmth of his strong hands, she was pulled in two directions—swept up in a sensual memory she wanted more of, and also wary of the ways he could affect her so easily.

"I'm glad," he said softly. "Until tomorrow, then. Good-bye, Kate."

"Good-bye," she said, trying to ignore the small inner voice that was saying, *Watch out, he's turning very tempting again. And he's too good to be true.*

The next day, a bit after ten, Kate was sitting at her desk trying to relax. She had tried on four different outfits that morning, angrily telling herself that her complete indecisiveness had nothing to do with Ben. But it was one of those days when absolutely nothing looked right or even half-decent. Finally she had settled on a forest-green silk button-down dress with short sleeves, something she knew looked good even though she didn't feel that way. Now, as she sat at her desk, she resisted the impulse to take out her compact to see how she looked. For she knew that in her current mood, she would think she looked terrible no matter what the reality was. She would feel her hair was too straight, her lips were too full, that her skin looked too pale next to green silk. And she didn't need to be any more ill at ease than she already was.

When the intercom on her desk buzzed, she jumped, and a few moments later Linda was ushering Ben into the office. He looked handsomer than Kate remembered, with his warm, smiling eyes and wonderfully relaxed and rugged air.

He glanced at Kate, then thanked Linda and shut the door. When he turned to Kate, he smiled. She thought he looked magnificent. "Good to see you," he said. "And so soon."

"Listen. It wasn't an easy fight. If I hadn't been almost obnoxiously persistent, the account would have gone to someone else."

He pursed his lips and looked at her thoughtfully. "I'm sure you were persistent. Obnoxious I doubt. But I'm sorry to hear you had trouble," he said as he put his briefcase and a paper bag down on the conference table. "What was the problem?"

"Oh, everything," she said, coming over to where he

stood. "I'd say that the objections were more politically based than anything else."

"That's right," he said. "I forgot you've just been promoted. Well. I promise," he said, stepping forward and putting his hands at her waist. "I promise that you'll never be sorry you decided on Blake-Canfield."

Fighting with herself, she reached down and took his hands from her waist. "Please," she said quietly, looking into his eyes and resisting their liquid softness. "Just—let's back up a little bit—for the moment."

He looked at her questioningly and she turned away, sitting down before she began to speak again. "I know," she began slowly, as he pulled out a chair and sat down beside her, "that I wasn't exactly cold to you the other day." She glanced at him then. He looked very serious, and she went on. "I don't like to give double messages. It's a habit of mine, I'm afraid. But in the end, it doesn't get anyone anywhere. So I want to be straightforward with you, Ben. Let's just agree—for now—that we'll slow down, and back off a bit."

He smiled. " 'We.' That's a nice way of putting it."

She shrugged. "It's true. Why should I be naive and pretend I have nothing to do with what's happening between us—that I'm an innocent who doesn't know what's going on?"

"Many women do just that."

"Well, I used to. But not anymore."

He looked into her eyes. "Have you made any decisions? About—what was his name—Kurt?"

She nodded, trying to read his tone, wondering whether he was really as concerned or caring as he sounded. How could he be, when he didn't even know her? "Look," she said. "Your asking me that is just the kind of thing I'm talking about. Let's just forget girl friends, boyfriends, past loves, future loves, and concentrate on trying to get some work done."

For a moment the amber of his eyes flashed into gold reflecting his deepening interest. They held her in thrall, telling her she was making a foolish mistake by protesting. And she wondered. For when she gazed into those eyes, she imagined them as they would be if she were in Ben's arms, his lips ready to melt with hers, his gaze as smooth and strong as silk.

As he looked at her, saying nothing, she resisted the impulse to tell him to forget what she had said; she fought against her natural desire once again to touch him, if only for a moment; she held herself—body and mind, impulse and words—in check.

And then he spoke. "I'm not going to sit here as we work together in the coming weeks and pretend that I'm not curious about you. Nor am I going to sit here and pretend I'm not interested. What if we both pretended—and we parted, in the end, never knowing what we might have meant to each other?"

She smiled. "That's a point. But really—I *don't* know you, Ben. I don't even know if you're married, for God's sake."

He tilted his head. "Do I act married?"

She laughed. "In a way, yes."

He didn't smile. "When I *was* married," he said slowly, "and I don't mean to sound sanctimonious—but I did not act as I have with you. In the first years of my marriage I never even looked at another woman."

"And then what happened?" she asked quietly.

"Something I'll never let happen again. We drifted apart, as they say. It's such an overused expression that it sounds trite, only partially true. But that was exactly what happened, in the most classic of ways. We had our kids, Eliza and Christopher, only a year and a half apart. From the moment Eliza was born—and then Christopher, so quickly afterward it seemed like weeks—we did nothing but talk about the kids. I went to work—I was a teacher then—came home, and from the moment I was home until I left the next morning, all that was on either of our minds was the kids. We stopped talking, really. We were both reciting, going through questions and answers, litanies of the day. I'd tell her a few things about work, she'd tell me a few things about the babies, and we might as well have been talking to walls, though neither of us noticed because we were so damn wrapped up in our problems. We caught ourselves when I decided to try my hand at advertising. I think Eliza was three at the time."

"Why did you switch?" Kate asked, settling more comfortably back in her chair.

"Money," he said simply. "I was already working a twelve-hour day. And I knew we weren't going to be able to raise two kids the way I wanted to on my salary."

"Are you sorry you switched?"

"Sometimes, yes. I went back to teaching after Celia and I were divorced. She was working by then and refused anything but child support." He paused and took out his pipe. "But anyway," he said, packing the sweet-smelling tobacco in and then lighting it, "it worked for a while again, when I began in the ad business. We thought of it as a new beginning, and we acknowledged that we needed one. But it never did work after that." He puffed on his pipe, and then smiled, his eyes flickering with warmth. "So much for getting down to business," he said. "How did we get on to marriage?"

She smiled. "You were telling me that you never looked at another woman at the beginning of your marriage."

"Well, I seem to have taken us off track once again." He smiled. "Maybe we should actually get started."

He took out two cups of coffee he had brought in a paper bag—a nice and surprising touch, she felt—along with the layouts Tommy Sullivan had sketched out, and they set to work. He began by reviewing the basic concept—talking quietly, slowly, intensely. He was relaxed but totally absorbed, and as Kate listened and occasionally questioned him, she was silently congratulating herself for having been wise enough to choose Ben Austin's campaign. Without him it would have been very, very good. With him and all the attention and enthusiasm he would bring to it, it was destined to be nothing short of wonderful.

They worked hard until lunch, and Kate was annoyed to find that it was she, not he, who tended to break the businesslike mood. She was constantly breaking her promise against giving double messages. When he would look up from a chart or sketch or layout he was showing her, she would catch his gaze in a look that said not, "How interesting," or "I agree," or anything relating in any way to what he had said. All she said with her eyes was "I want you." At those moments he tried to fight back. At the beginning, at least. He would look away as if he hadn't seen, or look at her in reproach and surprise, as if to say,

"I'm keeping up my end of the bargain. Why can't you?" Yet, for a reason she couldn't fathom, she kept it up: simmering glances, gentle touches on the hand or knee, her softest, lowest, most bedroom-seductive voice.

When the intercom buzzed and she rose to answer it, she silently warned herself that when she returned to Ben's side, she would be wise to cool down. And, for a few moments, as Linda told her she was going to lunch, Kate was distracted from Ben and her apparently uncontrollable behavior. But once she hung up and returned to the table, she could feel herself—with one glance at Ben—slip back into her most seductive of roles.

"That was Linda," she said. "Going to lunch. I hadn't realized it was so late."

He smiled. "Time flies when you're breaking your promise."

Her lips parted and then curved into a smile. "Ah. Not too subtle, then."

He laughed. "Very subtle. Very lovely. But sometimes things that are very subtle and very lovely have a very strong impact." He inhaled deeply. "For instance—that perfume you were wearing the other day. It was gentle, almost not there. At one moment I would sense it, and at the next, wonder if it had just been my imagination. But that night, when I closed my eyes and thought of you, Kate, I knew that every part of you, every aspect of you, had been real." He reached out and gently stroked her hand. Each stroking movement sent a rolling wave of warmth through her, a hazy heat that made her feel heavy with longing.

She gazed at him with a lazy half-smile. "Now I'm not

the only one breaking the promise."

He grinned. "But you started it. Which, as it turns out, is as meaningless a phrase as it is in childs' fights—because it could have been me." His hand moved upward, making hot, lazy circles along her arm, and she found herself leaning toward him, lips parted in desire, breathless. "And I hope you know that the reason I tried so very hard to resist," he murmured, his warm fingers moving over from her arm to the sensitive skin of her neck, "is that I just wanted to please you," he whispered.

Please me, she thought. Oh, God, she wanted him to, but not by staying away.

As she gazed into eyes of liquid honey, she was seared by the movement of his fingers just inside her collar. His fingers were warm, persuasive, and her breath quickened as his touch grew warmer. She could barely find her voice through thickening layers of desire. "And are you still trying to please me?" she whispered.

"I can think of nothing better," he said huskily.

For one moment their gazes were locked in a searing, breathless hold. And then, just as she wondered how long she would be able to wait, his hand at the back of her neck began to urge her forward, and his lips met hers in a blazing touch of exquisite lightness and intoxicating pleasure. His mouth on hers was warm, sweet, urgent, with the promise of unending passion. And then, somehow already attuned to each other's needs and wants and pleasures, they deepened the kiss together, lips parting in a moan of shared wonder and desire.

A fierce warmth spread through her body, igniting into a deep fire within her. The swiftness of her response was frightening and exhilarating at the same time, for somewhere in the back of Kate's mind was the thought *This is only a kiss—how can I be responding so deeply?* But her body had no questions, no doubts—only a smoldering certainty of coursing desire that craved this man in a much, much deeper way.

He tore his mouth from hers and looked at her with stormy eyes. "I've made a mistake," he murmured huskily, his breath coming quickly.

"What do you mean?" she asked, still hazy and reeling from the pleasures of his lips.

"I had thought that perhaps we'd see—that we'd kiss, and all the undercurrents we've been fighting against wouldn't be there after all. But . . . Kate."

She smiled lazily.

His face was close to hers—inches from her own—and she loved the scent that had intoxicated her moments before, the closeness of his hazel eyes, the feel of his breath soft against her cheek.

"You know what this means," he said quietly, drawing her to him once again for a gentle kiss.

Her senses were filled with exhilaration and desire, and with wonder as well—for she wondered at this man whose most gentle of touches could fill her with such pleasure.

He drew back, eyes serious. "Do you?" he asked.

"Do I what?" she asked dreamily, her voice barely there.

"Do you know what this means?" he asked, smiling.

She answered with a smile of her own. "No. Tell me what you think this means," she said playfully.

"It means there's no turning back," he said quietly.

For a moment she reveled in his gaze—in the obvious longing, the clear appreciation, the humor lurking just below the surface. "Tell me more," she said.

And then, inexplicably, his smile faded. "I'm serious, actually," he said. "And you may not even like what I'm going to say."

She frowned. "Maybe not. You're making me very nervous all of a sudden."

He put a hand under her chin and then held it against her cheek. "Don't be," he said tenderly. "It's just that we probably have trouble on our hands. All your talk about backing up and backing off obviously did no good. Look at us. And I want to respect your wishes, Kate—to do what you want. But Lord—do you honestly think that now we can back off? I just can't quite imagine sitting here talking with you over the next few weeks without wanting you." He smiled. "And I don't mean it in the 'mad lust' sense, as if I'm some teen-aged kid who's just discovered sex. I *do* mean it, Kate, but in a much subtler, I hope more meaningful, way."

She laughed. "Well! I'm glad to know I don't have a sex-starved teen-ager on my hands."

He pursed his lips. "Now, wait a minute," he said, trying to suppress a smile. "I don't want you going and thinking the opposite, Kate. My point was—"

"Understood," she finished for him. "And really, Ben," she said, looking into his eyes, "I have no idea what to say. I love everything you've said. I loved kissing you just now—obviously. But I just . . . don't feel I know anything. *I* don't know how we're going to work together over the next few weeks. We'll just have to see." And, though she had just finished giving a very neutral, cautioning little speech, only moments later she was taking in his handsome features with her most seductive of glances.

And she realized that somewhere along the way, she had lost control of her impulses and feelings and actions. Because no matter how cautious she had determined to be, she was falling very rapidly into the silken net of Ben's charms.

CHAPTER THREE

Later that afternoon, right after Ben left, Linda buzzed Kate on the intercom. "Kurt Reeves has been calling all day. Do you have a chance to talk to him now?"

Kate sighed. "Sure. Anyone else?"

"Uh, yes. Mr. Dayton."

"Great. What did he want?"

"You're asking me?" Linda laughed. "Kate, I'm just a secretary—how could I be trusted to pass along any information?"

Kate laughed. "Mm—that *is* his attitude, isn't it? Well, I'll give him a call and find out."

"Do you want me to get him for you?" Linda asked.

"Uh, no. I'll call Kurt first. But thanks."

She hung up and sighed. Kurt. She didn't know if the thought of calling him was especially unpleasant because of him, or because of the contrast to Ben. For she knew the call would be among her last with him—on a personal basis, at least. She didn't even want to think about what it would be like working with him from now on—one of the reasons she shouldn't, perhaps, have become involved with him in the first place.

And she was going to do it all over again with Ben

Austin, most likely: make the same mistakes, suffer the same shock of surprise, and then endure the difficulties that went along with continuing to work together. Yet, for all her attempted rationality, she couldn't imagine that the problems she'd have to expect in working with Kurt from now on would ever occur with Ben. Not that he seemed like a saint; but he seemed so . . . she hesitated. She couldn't quite put her finger on it. He was appealing in a thousand ways—handsome, sexy, sincere, attractive, intelligent—all qualities she had known in many men. But there was something extra that somehow found its way into all his other good qualities. And then she realized what it was. He was secure. Unlike Kurt, he didn't seem to need to have his ego stroked by every passing female; he didn't have a chasm of insecurity beneath his confident exterior. Unlike other men she had known, he didn't seem to have to prove himself in any way with her: intellectually, physically, emotionally. And she knew that, as he himself had said, there was no turning back.

If she could have had any confidence in her feelings, she would have been happy: she had, after all, apparently come across a very interesting, available man. But instead, the pleasure of anticipation was mixed with apprehension. For she feared that Ben would inevitably turn out like all the rest. It was just a matter of time.

In the meantime, however, she would do well to take advantage of her clearheadedness and break off the relationship with Kurt once and for all. There were no unanswered questions there, no mysteries yet to unfold.

She picked up the phone before she could procrastinate any longer. And in moments she was talking to Kurt.

"You called," she began.

"Yes. Several times, Kate. You've been in a hell of a long meeting."

"Yes, well, the new account executive and I had a lot to discuss."

"From Blake-Canfield? I just got the memo."

"It looks as if we're going to have a great campaign."

"That's great," he said. "But listen. I don't want to talk about that. I want to get together with you."

She sighed. "I really don't think there's much point, do you?"

"Why not?" he demanded. "You've kept me in the dark for days, Kate—some reference to something I don't even know about."

"Oh, come on!" she cried. "You want it spelled out, Kurt? Fine. It's over between us, you're seeing another woman, it would have been over anyway, and that's that. Okay?"

"I'm not seeing another woman," he said.

"Fine," she said. "I really don't care either way."

"What did you hear?"

"I heard you were seeing Cynthia Williston."

He didn't say anything. Then she heard him sigh. "I'm not seeing her anymore," he said. "You haven't even given me a chance to tell you that, you know. All of this is after the fact."

"Oh, come on. What difference does that make?"

"I'd like to see you," he said. "I think we could clear things up."

"I think we could cloud things up," she said.

"You know what, Kate?" he said in a low, angry voice she had never heard before. "I don't even know why I'm arguing. There are plenty of women who aren't hung up on monogamy the way you are."

"Fine," she said. "Go find them."

"I will," he answered. "But you know what?"

"What?"

"You're fooling yourself," he said heatedly, "into thinking you're something you're not—a woman who's interested in things like faithfulness and all that other stuff—for whatever reason—something in your background, I guess. But you're not really interested in any of that crap. Because if you were—really—you never would have hooked up with me in the first place. You're just playing games, Kate, like women who invite a man up to their apartments and are surprised when he makes a move."

"Well," she said quietly. "That's all very interesting. If you really think all of that, Kurt, then there really isn't any more to say. Good-bye." And she hung up. God! He had become so ugly! She knew that he had done so only because he was hurt, and angry. But she also knew that he had meant every word he had said. He had kept those thoughts to himself in the past, for obvious reasons. But the moment he knew the relationship was over—really over—he let her know what he really thought.

And the worst part was that much of what he had said was true.

She turned away from the phone and looked up Mr. Dayton's extension. If nothing else, he would distract her from thinking about Kurt.

"Kate," he said jovially, when she was finally put through by his secretary. "Thanks for returning my call. How's the campaign going?"

"Fine so far," she said. "It looks very, very promising."

"That's just great," he said. "And that's why I was calling. I'll tell you what. I think I may have something—or some*one*, I should say—who might be able to help you out. Really give the campaign some zing."

"Oh?" she said coolly, knowing she was bordering on rudeness but unable to muster any enthusiasm. It didn't sound promising, coming from him.

"Yes. Kate, I'll tell you what. If you have some time free, I'd like to bring her by your office. You can chat, get to know each other a little, and then tell me what you think."

She hesitated, waiting for him to say more, but apparently he had said all he was going to. "I'm sorry, Mr. Dayton. I don't quite understand. Who—uh, how is this person going to fit into my campaign?"

He chuckled. "I thought you'd never ask, Kate. As the Ivorsen and Shaw girl, naturally. My niece, Alexandra. She's just in from Kansas—this month, as a matter of fact. Been staying with the wife and myself, plans on getting her own place soon. Hitting the modeling agencies at this very moment, as a matter of fact. And you never did see a prettier twenty-one-year-old young woman, I swear. I think you'll love her."

Kate closed her eyes. She didn't need this at all. "Uh, Mr. Dayton, I'm sure your niece is very pretty. But the agency is handling the casting, and—"

"Now, look here," he interrupted, "Kate Churchill, I was in your office not more than twenty-four hours ago when you explained the *en*tire way the campaign was going to work. And you and I both know that if you wanted to cast King Kong's mother as the Ivorsen and

Shaw girl, you could. It's our campaign, Kate—not Blake-Canfield's."

She sighed. "Of course it's our campaign. But the campaign, sir, is an integral whole. All the parts have to fit together." As she spoke into what felt like a void, she realized she was taking an approach that wasn't quite right. She'd never be able to convince him to leave the campaign alone. And who knew, anyway? Maybe his niece would somehow—miraculously—be right for the part. "Please don't misunderstand me, Mr. Dayton. I'd love to meet your niece. And perhaps we can use her for other work, if she's not exactly right for the major campaign. In any case, all I meant was that I am working with Blake-Canfield Advertising, and I wouldn't want to do any hiring or even considering without them. But I'll tell you what. We're having an audition tomorrow—at the agency. Why don't you ask your niece to meet me there? And then we can see what develops."

"That sounds perfect," he said, obviously mollified.

She gave him the details, hung up, and then shook her head. Since yesterday, she had been expecting Dick Dayton to be difficult over the course of the campaign. But she hadn't anticipated what had just occurred. Now, if she didn't hire his niece—a distinct and likely possibility—he would be hypercritical for the duration of the campaign. And if she *did* hire his niece—extremely unlikely, but a possibility nonetheless—her authority would probably be challenged whenever Dick Dayton decided his dear little niece needed more exposure. Damn.

The next day Kate arrived at Blake-Canfield's offices on Fifty-fifth and Madison at eight forty-five. The audition was scheduled for nine o'clock, but Kate had taken a taxi to be sure she'd be on time, and it had miraculously zipped through traffic twice as quickly as Kate had expected.

After finding out from the receptionist that Ben wasn't in yet, Kate sat down on one of the low leather couches near the door. It was an impressive office, with soft lighting, cream-colored walls and carpeting, and large, blown-up prints of some of Blake-Canfield's ads. As Kate was wondering which ones Ben had worked on, a very pretty dark-haired young woman came in and walked over to the receptionist.

Kate hoped she was one of the auditioners. If she wasn't, Kate was going to seriously consider suggesting that she audition. There was something startling about the young woman, and that was the very quality Kate felt was most important in casting the ad. They didn't want faces that were too beautiful, off-putting to all but the most confident viewers. But they did want attractive. Special people with flair. And this young woman—dressed all in white, from her cowboy hat to her jeans to her boots—had a definite flair. Her hair was auburn, her eyes dark blue, and her skin was fair and smooth. And though her features were unusual—a full mouth, high cheekbones, high forehead—she was arrestingly pretty. And then Kate heard her give her name to the receptionist: Alexandra Dayton.

A few moments later, when she sat down near Kate, Kate introduced herself. They talked for a bit—about Alexandra's search for an apartment, about the modeling business and Alexandra's dread of the audition—and Kate found her natural and charming. When other people finally began filing in—employees, actors and actresses for the audition, messengers—Kate and Alexandra wound the conversation down. And then Ben strode in—his hair windblown, his cheeks red from the autumn chill. He lit up when he saw Kate. "Come on in to my office," he said, smiling. And she went with him down the long hall to his office.

It was the first time Kate had seen it, and she loved it immediately. It was very spare and businesslike, leaving the focus of the room to the magnificent view that swept down Madison Avenue. The furniture was all modern—deep, rich brown leather couches and chairs, sleek black desk and conference table. And there were more poster-size framed ads on the cream-colored walls.

When Ben closed the door softly behind him, Kate turned and looked at him, suddenly unaware of the surroundings, aware only that she was alone with him.

He looked wonderful. With his sheepskin jacket and corduroy pants he was a man with his own style—not like the hordes of Burberry-coated men rushing up and down Madison and Park avenues every morning.

His lips curved into a crooked, amused smile. "Am I wearing pajama bottoms?" he asked, looking downward. When he looked back at Kate, it was with a sparkle in his eyes. "You're looking at me as if I forgot something very crucial."

She laughed. "No, no. I was just—staring, maybe—because I liked what you were wearing. Not the usual successful-man-working-on-Madison-Avenue outfit."

He smiled. "Good." He tilted his head and looked at her speculatively. "But you know me better than that." He smiled. "I hope I'm more of a man going against the grain," he said, looking into her eyes. He came up close to her then, and put his hands warmly and temptingly over her hips. "I'm so glad to see you, Kate," he said softly.

He leaned forward and brushed his lips against hers. She pulled him closer, wrapping her arms around him and opening her lips to the delicious warmth of his tongue. What she loved most about kissing him was the way every moment was deep with need, the way he seemed to want her so very, very much. And he wanted to please her as well, kissing her deeply but gently, deepening the kiss only when she wanted more. With a moan that rose from deep inside she drew him in, tasting him with an ecstasy of pleasure, reveling in the heat that was enveloping them both.

Then slowly, gently, he drew back. "Kate," he whispered. And then he smiled broadly, hazel eyes shining with pleasure. "We do have to stop meeting like this, you know. Cliché or not."

She raised her chin and smiled. "What did you have in mind?"

"Oh, dinner. Dancing. Making love."

He brought his mouth down on hers then, in a long, deep kiss that spread pulsating heat through her body, weakening her limbs, firing her with a core of yearning that burned deep inside. He tasted wonderful, and she wanted more. She wanted to feel his warm skin against her own, to feel his slim hips against hers, to feel his long, muscular legs parting her own.

He drew back and his amber eyes searched hers. "When?" he asked.

She said nothing—she could say nothing, with her voice caught inside, under layers of desire.

"When?" he repeated, and she was suddenly aware of the hardness of his thighs, and a wild liquid warmth plunged through her body. "Tonight?" he murmured.

She smiled dreamily and said, "Yes."

He reached up and stroked her cheek with the back of his warm hand, and she inhaled his scent, brushing her lips across his skin.

He smiled.

"What?" she asked quietly.

"I'm just thinking about how we're in here enjoying ourselves and we're keeping two dozen nervous young kids out there quaking." He brushed back a strand of her hair. "I don't know how I'm going to be able to concentrate with you at my side." He took a deep breath. "I guess that's what casting directors are for."

She widened her eyes. "Getting derelict in your duties already, just because of a little personal influence?"

He smiled. "Don't worry. When I first met you and said that your account would be important to me, Kate, I meant it." He smiled into her eyes. "But if we're ever going to go out there, I think we should go now."

"Just one more kiss," she murmured, lips close to his.

He smiled, a look of pleasant surprise in his eyes. And then he tantalizingly brushed his lips across hers and winked. "They'll all be too old for the call by the time we get out there."

She laughed. "Okay. But, oh, I have to tell you something." She explained Alexandra Dayton's presence, leaving out her opinion about the young woman for the moment. She wanted to see what Ben and the casting director had to say about her first, and she also had some serious concerns about hiring her.

Kate and Ben went down to the casting room together, met with Andrew Coates, Blake-Canfield's casting director, for a few minutes, and waited while Coates went and brought the auditioners in. Coates was a young, slightly whiny man, good-looking until he began to speak. But Kate was impressed with the way he discussed the campaign, and from the looks of the auditioners she had seen out in the reception area, he had fairly good taste.

After Coates left, Kate looked around at the rows of beautifully cushioned seats, the slightly raised area at the far end of the room that apparently served as a stage, at the bare walls and floors that wouldn't afford perhaps-needed distractions to the anxious performers. There was video equipment everywhere, with a glassed-in control room at the back of the room and several cameras and microphones on and near the stage. She and Ben sat in the middle row of seats, and she imagined how threatening they probably would look from onstage: the client and the account executive, there to criticize, perhaps encourage in minor ways, but probably not to hire.

A few minutes later the door opened, and a stream of young men and women poured in, followed by Coates and a young woman with a clipboard. As Kate settled back to listen to Coates give his spiel, she was once again impressed. Ben had obviously conveyed the sense of the campaign quite well; and many of the concepts in it were less than obvious. Coates went on with some specific points about the script, a few hints about relaxing, and then called the first names.

Kate's stomach jumped as if the names were her own. And then, what seemed like only seconds later, Andrew Coates was thanking the first two auditioners as they stepped off the stage, and Kate realized she had missed their performance. And she wondered why she was so nervous. She was utterly distracted, completely in a daze. And then she remembered: just before the audition, she had agreed to see Ben tonight. In a dreamy, sensuous, lazy haze, she had said yes to more than just seeing him. She had said yes to much, much more.

As she felt Ben's presence next to her, knew every inch of him without even looking, a surge of pleasure erupted inside her, a thrill of anticipation that nearly made her tremble. And this, she realized, was what was sending bolts of fear through her. For her feelings for Ben were so strong—physically and emotionally—that she felt she had lost control.

She had thought of her answer as an act of strength, as an aspect of being a woman who could make choices and decisions and take actions others might consider premature or impetuous. She was her own woman, beholden to no one, and she could do what she wanted. But underneath this confidence and self-determination, underneath the wonderful feeling she'd had when she had breathed yes against Ben's lips was the fear that she wasn't really in control, and now she was swept with doubt.

Kate tried to concentrate on the auditions. As they went on with faltering lines, misinterpreted inflections, halting movements, Kate's heart went out to the auditioners; but she was viewing it all dispassionately as well, interested more in the performances than in the actors' hopeful, tentative smiles and gentle looks of disappointment as they left the stage.

And she was amazed that her initial intuition about Alexandra Dayton had turned out to be correct: she was a shining star among amateurs, someone who made her otherwise unremarkable partner shine as well. Within moments this rather dull young man had a sparkle in his eye and a verve in his voice that had been absent only seconds before. Alexandra Dayton was clearly one of those performers who could imbue her partner, if only temporarily, with the same magic she possessed herself. And Kate wanted her for the campaign. Yet she had questions and qualms. Alexandra Dayton was Dick Dayton's niece. What if there were problems, and they had to fire the young woman from the campaign? Kate had an instinct: right now, freedom in the campaign was of the utmost importance. Yet, as she looked at Alexandra, at the young woman's obvious beauty and presence, she wondered whether she wasn't in fact being too cautious; taking chances was what success in business was all about. She simply didn't know. . . .

After Alexandra and her partner had finished, Ben leaned over to Kate and whispered, "No question—she's the one."

"I have some questions," she said quietly. "We'll talk about it later."

Kate watched the rest of the auditions carefully, trying to keep an open mind about the rest of the performers. But it didn't take much effort or discernment; there were two different leagues at work—amateur and professional—and Alexandra Dayton was the only member of the latter group. Which meant that Kate had to make a tough decision.

After all the auditioners had left, Ben and Kate moved to the front of the room and sat down with Coates and his assistant.

Ben lit his pipe, leaned back, and looked at Kate and Andrew. "No question in my mind. We have one call-back and one call-back only. Alexandra Dayton. The rest we can forget about for now."

Andrew Coates nodded. "Agreed by me. That girl was spectacular." The young woman at his side nodded.

Ben looked at Kate. "Kate?"

She sighed. "I agree, except for the fact that she's Dick Dayton's niece. It makes me nervous."

"She was perfect, Kate," Ben said.

"I agree," she said. "There was no comparison—and I'm sure that would be true in future auditions. But I just have a feeling. An intuition."

Ben looked at her carefully. "Perhaps we'd better discuss this ourselves, Kate," he said coldly, "and let Andrew and Laura get back to their other work." He stood up. "Andrew, Laura, I'll talk to you before the day is out." And he motioned for Kate to come with him.

She said good-bye to Andrew and Laura and followed Ben out, furious that he had ended the meeting so abruptly. And she was furious at herself for not having said anything.

They went into his office, now flooded with midmorning sun, and Ben closed the door.

"Is something wrong?" he asked, coming over to where she stood by the window. He smiled. "Did I detect waves of anger coming from you as we walked down the hall, or was that just my imagination?"

She smiled at the description, but grew serious again. "I *am* angry, Ben. Because of—because of our relationship, you seem to think that you can speak for me, make my decisions for me, cut me off. . . ." Her voice trailed off. He looked mystified, and she was suddenly unsure of her words.

"Why?" he asked. "Because I give my opinion, and advise you as I'm supposed to? And because I save time by talking with you myself instead of having everyone in the agency in on it? Kate, I'm just doing my job." He reached out and stroked her cheek with the back of his hand. "And I'm doing it as well as I possibly can—because of my feelings for you."

"But you don't even listen to what I'm saying. You were so sure back there in the casting room that Alexandra Dayton was perfect that we didn't even get a chance to discuss any of the others."

He drew his head back in surprise and took his hand away from her cheek. "The others? What others? Alexandra Dayton or not, they weren't right for call-backs—and you know that."

For a few moments there was silence. Kate looked out the window, Ben looked at Kate. When she turned and met his eyes, she was swept with confusion. He was so wonderful-looking, with his deep, dark-lashed eyes, the smile lines at the corners that made her want to smile herself, his easy masculinity. It was so easy to like him. But when he went against her, as now, it made her realize how little she knew him: his warmth and affection were not all that he was made up of. She was being swept along a river whose direction she didn't know.

She looked out the window again, as if the outer world would give her strength for what she had to say. "I don't think we should see each other tonight," she said quietly.

'Why not?"

She turned and faced him. "It's . . . interfering already.

I'm sure you see that. And you yourself have said that this campaign is of critical importance because it's the first one I've been in charge of at I and S." She sighed. "Don't you see?"

"I see that you're not telling me something," he said quietly. "And that's certainly your prerogative. But I wish you would be honest, Kate. You know as well as I that my liking you—and being interested in you—hasn't interfered with anything one bit. So it must be something else." He looked into her eyes. "That first thing that comes to mind is that you're just not interested."

Her heart jumped; he had to know that wasn't true. "That isn't it," she said. "Believe me."

"Is it that you want to be friends only?" he asked softly.

She caught his gaze in hers. "You know that's not true," she answered.

"Then tell me, Kate—I'm not a mind reader."

He stepped forward and put his hands at her waist.

"Don't," she said, but she felt herself say yes with her eyes in delicious and eager acquiescence. And moments later his lips were on hers, covering them with warmth, filling her with desire until she parted her lips and welcomed the sweetness of his tongue.

Oh, God, she thought. *Save me from this desire, this need, this man.* She melted under his touch, bringing her body up to his, wanting to feel the hardness of his frame. Her hands slid hungrily along his back, moving up to his hair and plundering it with heated pleasure. She wanted to explore every part of him, to possess him completely. For she could feel his desire was as strong as her own, that he shared her wonder over the swiftness and depth of their passion.

She tried to think of what she had meant to say, of what she had thought only moments before. But all she knew was that there was no fighting this utter melting in Ben's arms. This was something new, something she had never before experienced, even in her most intimate moments. From the deepest, most fiery core of her soul, she needed this man. And as his lips and tongue played with hers, as his expert hands roved along her hips and around her waist, she knew there was no resisting him.

When he lifted his mouth from hers, his eyes were dark with desire. "I can't force you to tell me what's wrong, Kate," he rasped. "I can ask, and hope that you'll tell me because you feel the way I do—that we could have something very, very special if you would let it happen. And I can't change, or help, or do anything any differently, unless you tell me. I'm following your eyes, and your smiles, and all the cues I can follow. And they all tell me that when I take you in my arms, you want that. If I'm wrong, you have to tell me so."

"Oh, you're not wrong," she said breathlessly, still warm and aching inside from his touch. "I wish that you were—but you're not."

"Then, what is it?"

"I don't know what to say except to tell you the truth. I'm uneasy; I don't like this feeling I have when we're together, when I'm in your arms. I feel as if I've lost control."

A corner of his mouth lifted. "Don't you think I feel the same way?" he asked softly. "Why do you think I'm pursuing you like this? Don't you realize, Kate, you only feel this way when it's right—not when it's wrong?"

"I—I don't know," she murmured. She tried to think:

how had she felt with Kurt, and with the others? Had she felt this exhilaration, this heady whirl of emotions that threw reason to the winds?

"Trust me," he whispered. "And I promise you something, Kate Churchill. Tonight it's all up to you. I want to be with you where we don't have phones ringing every two minutes and people ready to come in at any moment. If I could"—he smiled—"I'd take you out to the countryside, to a mountain cabin where you wouldn't be able to think of anything *but* romance. But even then, Kate, I'd follow your lead. It will be a night just to talk, perhaps—with no advertising or retailing or office talk. That's the only rule. And we'll take it from there." He tilted his head. "If you're willing."

She looked away from him; she couldn't think straight when she was caught in the silken strands of his gaze.

"And if not," he said—she looked up, and he smiled—"if not, I'll just tote you up as hopelessly indecisive, and we'll forget the whole thing."

"You think you can goad me into it, don't you," she said, smiling.

His eyes sparkled. "Can I?"

She raised her brows and smiled in challenge. "Definitely not. And anyway, I forgot—it's Thursday night. The store is open late, and even though my staff goes home at five, I have to stay on."

"Why?"

"Oh, it's my own doing, actually. I was having an argument one day—when I was assistant director of advertising—with the head cosmetics buyers. And I said I thought the heads of departments should be more in touch with the buying public. It was a good idea, but half made up of spite. Anyway, it became store policy a few weeks ago. And now we circulate through the store and talk to customers on a one-to-one basis." Kate shrugged. "Now I wish I had never suggested it; I was just trying to aggravate this woman. And there's no good reason the department heads can't do the same thing during the day."

Ben looked thoughtful. "I don't really know that that's true, Kate—you have an entirely different market at night. And I like the idea of getting out and meeting with the public. I like it a lot. I think we could do more with it."

"Great. I was just thinking of trying to abolish the damn thing."

Ben shook his head. "Uh-uh. Don't do a thing yet. But I'll tell you what. I'll call you later after I talk to Coates about the other auditions. And if it can't be tonight, I'll have to goad you into some other night."

She smiled as she gathered up her things and walked to the door. "Maybe," she said.

He shook his head, his eyes dark and serious. "No maybes, Kate. Not anymore."

And, as she looked at him one last time before she opened the door, she saw that he was dead serious.

CHAPTER FOUR

When Kate got back to her office that afternoon, there was a note on her telephone: CALL ME THE SECOND YOU GET IN! from Alison.

Alarmed, Kate picked up the phone and dialed Alison's extension before looking at the other messages Linda had left.

Alison was talking nonstop before Kate had finished saying hello: "What the hell happened at that audition?" she said. "This girl came flying past my office today in tears, and I found out afterward that it was Dick Dayton's niece crying her eyes out over the audition at Ben Austin's agency."

"What?" Kate said. "Why?"

"You tell me. I don't know. I got this from Joan Samuels, who got it from her secretary, who got it from Dayton's secretary, so what we're dealing with here might not be a hundred percent reliable. But from what I understand, she had thought she'd be chosen for the part—who the hell knows what that crazy Dick Dayton told her?—and then you and Austin and the rest of the agency people didn't say a word when she was finished. I don't know, Kate—she might even still be in Dayton's office. I saw them leave together for lunch, and I saw them come back a while ago."

Kate swore under her breath. "I knew this would happen," she said. "The fact is, Ally, that that girl was far and away the best of anyone we saw. We didn't tell her she was coming back because that's not the way it's done—we're calling people afterward. But I argued with Ben about hiring her—I knew there would be problems because of her connection with the store."

"Well, you've got them, Kate."

And then Kate saw the phone message at the top of the pile: "11:00: Dick Dayton. Urgent." Underneath, it said, "Dick Dayton—11:30 A.M.—Urgent."

"Listen," Kate said. "I'd better get off and call him before he has my head. There are two messages marked 'urgent' already."

"Okay. But wait one second," Alison said. "What about Ben? What's happening with the two of you?"

"I don't know, Alison," she answered, sighing. "I think I really messed it up. I'm so paranoid after Kurt and so indecisive that I just keep switching gears. I'm definitely driving him crazy."

"Oh, come on. From the way you've described him, Kate, he sounds very unrufflable. I'm sure you're not driving him crazy except in a good way."

"Well, everyone has his or her limits. Anyway, I'm driving myself crazy even if he's not bothered. Because, Ally, I really like him. That scares me, but it feels good, too."

She heard Alison sigh. "Then, go for it, Kate. Go for him."

Kate smiled. Suddenly, her only thought was *Why not?*

Why not, when she had made so many mistakes before? Why not, when he seemed so right? He *did* seem different from the others. Why couldn't she allow herself to try, at least? "I think I just might do that," she said quietly. "I really think I might."

A few moments later she said good-bye and dialed Dayton's extension.

"Dayton," he barked.

Bad sign, Kate thought. He hadn't even let his secretary pick up.

"Kate Churchill," she said.

Silence. Then: "Would you come in here for a moment, please?"

She bristled. True, had he been talking to a man at her corporate level he might have used the same words; but he definitely wouldn't have used such a commanding tone. "I'm free in half an hour," she said. "But I can talk for a moment. What can I help you with?"

"We'll discuss it when you come in," he said, and hung up.

Adrenaline raced through her. Damn him! And the worst part was that if she were angry with him when she went into his office, she would be called "emotional," a woman who "tends to fly off the handle." Whereas a man in the same situation would be called no-nonsense, or straightforward.

She worked her way down through the rest of the phone messages, and exactly forty minutes after she had spoken to Dayton, left her office. True, she could have left ten minutes earlier and been on time, but she could play the power game as well as the best of them, and damn well would. Dayton was one of the most devoted practitioners of office politics and power plays at the store. His desk faced the door of his office, and his back was to the large picture window behind his desk. With the window facing south, visitors were often forced to look at Dayton and squint into the sunlight. And even without the sunlight the picture was of a large man framed by the sky and Manhattan's magnificent skyline—a man of power in a city of power. But Kate found him among the easiest of the corporate higher-ups to deal with. For he was predictable where he thought he was savvy, dull and plodding where he thought he was quick.

Dayton kept her waiting—naturally. But she was finally shown in to his office, where she greeted Alexandra—sitting on the couch with her portfolio at her side—cheerfully, as if nothing in the world were wrong. Then she looked expectantly at Dayton. "You wanted to see me about the audition, I assume," she said, taking a seat and training her clear brown eyes on him with a steadiness that belied her true feelings.

He nodded, "Yes, Kate. And naturally, I would have rather met with you alone. But Alexandra wanted to hear what you had to say."

Kate knew she'd have to speak carefully. "About the audition—?"

Dayton nodded.

"I don't understand. Was there a problem?"

Dayton looked at her carefully. "You tell me."

"Not as far as I was concerned. Alexandra, you did a lovely job. You have an excellent future ahead of you."

Alexandra looked surprised. "You didn't say that at the agency," she said, her voice high and uncertain. Kate was amazed at how differently Alexandra acted when being herself rather than playing a part. She was shy, diffident, very uncertain of herself.

"No, I didn't," Kate said. "Any encouragement or calling back comes later, after we've had a chance to discuss each person's performance."

Alexandra's eyes widened. "Oh. You mean—you liked me?"

She sounded so sincerely innocent that Kate forgot her annoyance with Dayton and smiled. "Yes, of course. I'm sure we'll want to see you again." The girl's face lit up. "But that doesn't mean you'll be chosen," Kate hastily added. "I want to be sure you understand that."

Alexandra nodded quickly. "Yes, yes, I understand. Only, I hope—oh, well. I'm so glad," she said, smiling. "I thought you hated me. I'm sorry."

Kate glanced at Dayton. "Well, *I'm* sorry your uncle didn't explain the situation more clearly. But perhaps he didn't know, either." Dayton's lips tightened. "Which is understandable," Kate continued, "since advertising really isn't his field. But Alexandra, if you have any questions in the future, just ask me, all right?"

The young woman nodded. "I will. I will."

Dayton glared at Kate and then turned to his niece. "Honey, leave us alone for a few minutes, all right?"

"Sure," Alexandra said, and jumped up from the couch and left. And Kate realized once again that whatever problems existed with Dayton, one couldn't deny that his niece was as graceful as a dancer.

But the moment Kate looked back at Dayton and saw the belligerent glint of his eyes, she was ready for battle.

"You surprise me," he said, picking up a pen and twirling it, looking more at it than at Kate.

"Why is that?" she asked.

He took a deep breath. "You're raising that poor girl's hopes only to disappoint her in the future."

"Why do you assume she won't be chosen?" Kate asked.

"It's obvious, isn't it? If you had any intentions of hiring her you would have done so already. It would have been kinder to tell her the truth right out."

"I did tell her the truth," Kate said. "Whether you think so or not."

He leaned back and steepled his fingers over the desk. "My niece is very important to me, Miss Churchill. As you may or may not know, my wife and I have no children of our own. I wouldn't like to see Alexandra's feelings hurt."

"And I don't think *she'd* like to know you were making not-very-veiled threats on her behalf, Mr. Dayton. And I think I should tell you that whatever chances she does have for being selected are rapidly diminishing with every word you say. If I feel you're going to interfere with the campaign as you have with the auditions, that will be a very good reason not to hire your niece."

"Don't be unwise about this, Miss Churchill," he warned.

She stood up and smiled. "I don't intend to be," she said. "And if you have nothing else on your mind, Mr. Dayton, I do have other business to attend to."

She turned and left, knowing that he had his usual look of tight-lipped anger on as he sat at his desk. But she did have other things to do. And though she knew it wasn't wise to antagonize a board member, she felt she had acted fairly reasonably under the circumstances. She had been provoked, and she had responded as calmly as she had been able to.

Later that afternoon, not having heard from Ben about the rest of the auditions, Kate called his office. But he was out, so she left a message and got back to work. Despite the fact that the new campaign was beginning to shape up, she still had the daily routine of getting print ads out on time, and she was swamped with work.

By the time it was five o'clock, she still hadn't heard from Ben, and she was a bit annoyed. She had wanted to talk to him about the Alexandra Dayton matter, and though it could wait, it was something she wanted to settle quickly. She tried his office again, but this time was told that he had left for the day.

And, unfortunately, it was time to go down to the selling floors of the store and circulate. At the beginning, a few weeks before, Kate had enjoyed talking to the buying public. Finding out what they liked and hated was interesting and often fun; customers were generally pleased that someone was actually interested in what they thought, and they responded fully and enthusiastically. But tonight Kate was definitely not in the mood. The pressure was on as it had never been before for more customers; and for each person she would see in cosmetics or lingerie or Fifth Avenue fashions, she would be wishing deep down for ten more.

Before going downstairs, Kate checked herself in the mirror of the ladies' room. She had definitely looked better at nine that morning; but she did the best she could, brushing her hair, reapplying her lipstick and eyeliner, and adding a bit more perfume.

For a moment her heart fluttered as she remembered

what Ben had said about the scent—that it was lovely, subtle, something he had remembered when he was apart from her. And she wished that she were with him, in his arms instead of in some ladies' room putting on makeup under fluorescent lights.

Sighing, she left the ladies' room and went down the hall to the elevators; she'd do what she had done every Thursday night over the past weeks—start at the ground floor, where most of the customers were, and work her way up from there.

When the elevator doors opened, she drew in her breath and started. Ben was standing there, and he smiled and stepped out as if it were the most natural thing in the world that he had come.

"Ah. Just in time," he said, as he put his arms around her and kissed her lightly on the lips. "I rushed to get here."

She smiled and looked into his eyes. "I'm so glad. I was just thinking about you."

"I thought you might like some company." He smiled. "We might even do a better job of it together, you know."

"Great," she said. "Then, let's go. This might not be the most interesting evening you've ever spent, Ben, covering all the floors of this store, but I'm really glad you came." She turned to press the elevator button, but he caught her arm.

"Wait a minute," he said. When she looked into his eyes, they were shining with spirit. "Why do you say something like that? I came to be with *you,* Kate—and, I hope, to spirit you away afterward if you're not too tired. I'm not here by chance, or because I feel a great need to meet your customers. I'd like to, but that's secondary."

As he leaned downward, his eyes closing as his lips drew near, she wrapped her arms around him, and she tried to quell the small inner voice that wondered if Ben could possibly be real. She had decided to put her doubts aside, decided—finally—to open herself up to a relationship with him; yet now, once again, she was nagged by doubt. She had been wrong so many times. Every time. How could now be any different? But as his lips gently brushed hers, and she opened her eyes and looked into his filled with desire, wonder, and affection, she moaned and pulled him closer. Doubt was replaced by pleasure, uncertainty replaced by deep need, and she hoped, viscerally and as deeply as could be, that someday she would stop doubting Ben forever.

When he drew back, he smiled. "Kate Churchill, you're a liar."

Her eyes widened. "What? Why do you say that?"

"Because anyone who kisses like that and responds to me as you did now has to know what she means to me." He ran a hand along the length of her back, sending a tremor of pleasure through her. "And there's no use denying it. Your body doesn't lie."

She laughed. "Well. You might be right," she said lightly.

He shook his head. "You know damned well I'm right, Kate. I want you to see that."

She smiled. "Maybe I do," she said softly. "Maybe I do."

The next few hours were an unanticipated delight. Kate and Ben started at the ground floor of the store, made up of the usual perfume and cosmetics displays, along with the dozens of small boutiques that made Ivorsen and Shaw special.

Together Ben and Kate talked to more people than in all the weeks Kate had been doing her Thursday-night tours. They went through the ground floor slowly, then through Nighttime Secrets lingerie and on to the men's-wear, resort-wear, and sporting-goods departments, then almost an hour in the home-gifts department. Kate had a better sense of the store's customers than she had ever had before; somehow, Ben managed to draw each one he talked to out of his or her shell. And after their initial surprise at being approached by anyone who wasn't a salesperson, most were more than forthcoming, welcoming Ben's form of indirect help and in turn helping him.

Finally, after they had talked to half a dozen people in the gifts department, Ben led Kate off to the store's restaurant, Il Trattoria. In addition to its small tables it had a counter where shoppers could get the restaurant's fare to take home. Decorated in clean, modern lines, with white tile floors and walls and butcher-block tables, the restaurant was a big draw for the store's customers. It had delicacies difficult to find even in New York—perfectly smoked molasses ham, the finest fresh Russian Malossol caviar, perfect *paté de canard,* three hundred kinds of cheeses—and it was all served and displayed absolutely beautifully, with the freshest of fruits and vegetables and breads almost everywhere one looked.

Now, all the tables were filled, but Ben led Kate to the small line of customers standing at the counter. "I assume we can eat in your office?"

She nodded.

"I had had other places in mind," he said, smiling, "but I suppose this will have to do."

"Oh, this place is great," she said. "I love it. And it's a perfect cure for the midtown lunch syndrome."

Ben smiled. "What's that?"

"Well, you probably don't know because you've always been at too high a corporate level to experience it. It happened to me when I used to be a secretary and it still happens when I'm in a rush. Basically, you go shopping or window-shopping, at the beginning of your lunch hour and then before you know it you only have half an hour left. So you go into restaurant after restaurant in the forties and fifties and at every single place, either the prices are too high, or there's a long line, or you sit at the counter and wait forever to be served. So you go back to the office with a container of yogurt and a cup of coffee and plan to move to another city. But with *this* place, you really can find something incredibly good for not that much money. And it's clean as well."

Ben was smiling. "And how many people know about this place, Kate?"

She shrugged. "We advertised in the newspapers when it first opened. But the board cut my budget; they felt the Trattoria wasn't big enough to devote that much ad money to."

Ben shook his head. "It may be the first department we advertise. Depending, my dear, on whether the food is truly as good as you say. Oh—by the way, Christina Casey over at my agency just finalized the arrangements for the campaign kickoff party. It will be at Xenon, downtown."

"That's wonderful!" Kate said. "I feel as if it's all starting to fall into place."

A few minutes later they were taking the employees' elevator up to the eighth floor, where Kate's office was, with bags filled with black forest ham, *pâté de campagne,* Jarlsberg, Montrachet, and Swedish fontina cheeses, Swiss peasant bread, Russian coffee cake, and fresh cold cider.

The halls were dark and quiet, lit only by red-and-white exit signs here and there.

"I'm glad you're here," Kate whispered, taking Ben's arm. "I hate coming up here after hours."

"You don't have to whisper," he said, smiling.

She laughed. "You're right. But I do feel as if we're sneaking around."

They reached her office, and she unlocked it and turned on the light. When they stepped inside, Ben closed the door and locked it, then took the bags and put them down on the conference table. Then he turned and took Kate in his arms, his strong hands deliciously warm at her waist, the pressure of his fingers sending a surge of pleasure through her. "Well, we *are* sneaking around, in a way," he said.

"Oh, really?" she asked, wrapping her arms around his neck. "I didn't know that."

He nodded, the light of mischief in his eyes. "Oh, yes," he said softly. "After all, you're getting paid to be downstairs, dutifully talking to your loyal customers—not up on the eighth floor enjoying yourself with me behind closed doors."

She smiled. "Locked doors, I hope."

"Oh, yes," he murmured. "But why the concern?"

His eyes were dark and cloudy with desire, heating her with need as she whispered, "Because I have an idea."

"And what is that?" he breathed, lips only inches from hers.

"Just this," she said softly, pulling him close as he lowered his mouth to hers. Her lips parted instantly and she moaned, eager for the sweetness of his mouth, the urgency of his tender lips. His tongue played with hers, entering her mouth, drawing her in to the depths of desire. The kiss was deep, smoldering, sending surging desire to the center of Kate's soul, heating her body in radiating waves.

"You look so beautiful tonight," he whispered. "God, Kate, to have you with me all evening without a touch." His fiery gaze roved downward. "You must have worn that dress to drive me crazy," he said huskily, moving his hands over the thin silk of her dress.

"I didn't know you were coming," she said, her voice thick with desire.

His fingers lightly circled, catching her nipples and tantalizingly moving on, and Kate warmed under his touch and the heat of his gaze: he took such obvious pleasure in her body, in her responses.

"You knew I'd come," he whispered. "You knew I'd come with the certainty my fingers have of you right now," he murmured. "And the certainty that's in your hands as you touch me, Kate, and know how quickly your touch arouses me."

"Ben," she murmured thickly as he pulled her against him. She felt the hardness of his frame and moved her hands over his back and down his sides. She parted her lips to receive his scorching kiss while his hands traveled over her shoulders and down to her hips. She could have him now, she realized. She could have this lean, strong man bring her to the heights of fiery pleasure, to the exploding pitch of ecstasy. She knew the satisfaction deep inside would be greater than any she had ever felt. He needed her—in the urgency that lay just beneath his tenderness, she felt a force that matched the strength of her own desire.

"Kate," he muttered, placing a warm hand on her thigh, caressing it and dissolving her into mindless passion as his fingers became more insistent against the material of her dress.

She reached for him. She felt the hard strength of his need tremble under her touch, and she achingly wished she could touch him, feel his heat, his strength inside, stroking and filling her with pleasure.

He moaned, his breath hot in her ear.

She could feel him holding back, feel the urgent need beneath her fingers. "Ben," she whispered. "I want you so much, but not here."

"Darling," he interrupted, gazing into her eyes. His breath was still coming fast, and his eyes were dark with passion. "Darling, it doesn't matter where we are, does it?"

"Yes," she murmured, the heat of her desire unwinding, spiraling down. "It matters to me. I wouldn't be able to let go, to really be with you."

He lowered his head and rubbed his sandy-rough cheek against hers. "Then we'll wait," he answered hoarsely. "I wouldn't want to make love with you unless you wanted it as much as I did, darling." He raised his head then, and looked at her with heavy-lidded eyes. "It's difficult for me to hold back when I want you as much as I do, but never—never would I make love to you except when you wanted me to."

"You know how much I want you." She smiled. "And how much I wish we were somewhere else right now."

He brushed a strand of dampened hair back from her forehead and kissed the spot where it had been. "Come to my apartment, then?"

She sighed. She wanted to so much. Physically, emotionally, in every way. Yet part of her held back. She looked into his clear amber eyes. "Ben," she began quietly, "I don't know how to say this. And I hope you understand when I do. But . . . when we're finally together, I want it to be spontaneous, something that absolutely must be, something completely unpremeditated." She looked at him wistfully. "I don't even know whether what I just said makes any sense. But it's the way I feel."

"It makes sense," he said quietly. "And I'm glad you said it, Kate. I want you always—always—to tell me how you feel. And I know that's difficult. It's difficult for me, too."

She smiled. "I have an idea," she whispered, warming once again to the feel of his body against hers, to the heat that was once again emanating from every inch of him. As she looked into his eyes, the ache inside her grew, knowing he was feeling as she did, knowing his desire was growing as quickly as hers.

"I hope it's the same one I have," he said, moving against her.

"Ben," she uttered, closing her lips over his. She had been planning to say she would go to his apartment later—if she wanted, as spontaneously as she could manage. But now she was awash in waves of overpowering longing, engulfed in fluid desire as she felt with every inch of her body what it would be like to make love with Ben. His desire was so obvious, his feelings so tender, so ardent, so generous. He was everything she had ever wanted. In her arms, ready to please her, ready to give, ready to bring her to the heights of pleasure and let her take him along the same fiery path.

"I've changed my mind," she said huskily. "I've changed my mind, Ben. Take me home with you."

CHAPTER FIVE

They left the store without looking back—talking to no one, saying good-bye to no one, thinking only of each other and the pleasures they were about to explore. Though she knew she was moving quickly as she and Ben left the store and walked out on to Third Avenue for a taxi, Kate felt languorous, almost as if she were walking in slow motion—moving out of pure instinct rather than conscious thought.

She and Ben said nothing as they waited for the taxi—but the gazes they shared when their eyes met went much, much deeper than words. He had his arm around her waist—protectively, possessively, out of sheer pleasure in the slightest touch. And as Kate looked up at his handsome profile, she felt that Ben might be the man she had been waiting for, the one she was meant for, the one she might be able to love as she had never loved before.

The feeling had crept up on her, unseen and unsensed because she had been so frightened and wary. He had surprised her because in so many ways, he was unpredictable. Even tonight, as Kate had gone around the store with him, he had surprised her—at one moment acting like the consummate playboy, charming a young woman into a near trance, but at the next helping out an old man as if the man were the most important person in the world. And she felt easy with him—as if he wouldn't pressure her; yet, when she was ready for him, he was hers with a force that showed he had held himself back with all his might.

But as she looked at him, with a tug of fear and sadness she realized there were many, many things she didn't know about him. Could she love him? And was he ready for love? He wanted her; but was he ready for all that went along with the fulfillment of that desire?

She shuddered involuntarily, and he pulled her closer. "Cold?" he asked, the light of affection and desire still bright in his eyes.

She smiled and shook her head, and slung her arm around him and held him close.

On the taxi ride to Ben's apartment on East Seventy-ninth Street, they talked quietly, sporadically, each lost in thought more than in conversation. Though there was little talk, Kate felt there was more communication, more connecting, than if they had spoken. For she knew, with the same deep certainty that told her he wanted her, that he was thinking about her. Thinking, wondering, perhaps wishing. And she wanted to keep everything just as it was, with no clouds on the horizon: just two people filled with possibilities, and questions that could be answered another time.

The taxi stopped at an impressive-looking prewar building, with a scallop-trimmed canopy over the entranceway and hedges to its sides. A uniformed doorman came to the curb to open the taxi the moment it pulled up, and soon Kate and Ben were walking through a beautiful lobby with marble floors, high, chandeliered ceilings, fine antique furniture, and gilt-framed oil paintings. The atmosphere somehow didn't quite fit Kate's image of Ben; she would have expected a more casual, less obviously monied building. But then, she reminded herself, Ben was a man of many paradoxes; and though he dressed very casually, he obviously did have money.

The apartment, one of two on the fifteenth floor, was another surprise. She had thought it would be modern and sleek like his office, perhaps with the stark emptiness that came after divorce. But it was the opposite: the foyer and living room were warm and cozy-looking, filled with antique oak and walnut furniture, old Americana, and beautiful braided rugs. Old posters and prints on the walls showed that Ben had spent much of his time antiquing, and everywhere Kate looked, there was something unusual and beautiful to look at: an old spice cabinet weathered with age, a simple painting of a village square, a rocker burnished golden from use.

She followed Ben into the living room and sat down on a fluff-filled couch that felt like a cloud. "This is so comfortable!" she said. "Where is it from?"

He smiled. "I had it specially made. My interest in antiques ends where the discomfort begins, and one day I thought, hell, I work hard enough, I can damn well come home and sink into something great. And this is the result."

"Well, it's wonderful," she said.

"How about a drink to go with it? Martini?"

"Great. How long have you lived here, by the way?" she asked as Ben went over to the small bar across the room.

"Oh, let's see. Fourteen years, I guess. We bought it when Eliza was two and Christopher was one."

"It's a coop?"

"Yes. And at the time it was way beyond our means. But I knew that we could manage—we would *have* to manage—if I made that kind of financial commitment, and we did. I wanted the kids to grow up in a nice neighborhood, and in a safe building." He smiled. "And for a time, they did."

He came back to the couch carrying a tray with two glasses and a pitcher, and he sat down. "Well. To us," he said, handing her a glass and then raising his own. He caught her in his gaze, and added, "I mean that."

She smiled and drank.

The liquid was warm, deliciously smooth as it spread its radiance through her body. She looked at Ben and smiled again, more lazily this time. "I love your apartment," she said. "But nice as it is, I'm surprised you kept it after the divorce." She paused. "I hope you don't mind my asking."

"Of course not," he said. "And please, Kate—never hesitate. I won't with you. Anyway, naturally I had thought of putting the apartment on the market when Celia and I separated. But I realized I loved it. It had happy memories as well as sad ones, and I felt that giving it up would be running away, trying to deny something that had once been very important. And I wanted a place the kids could stay when they visited."

"Do you see them often?"

He looked down into his drink for a moment. When he looked up, there was a vulnerability in those eyes that almost broke her heart. "Not as often as I'd like, naturally." He smiled. "I guess every divorced father feels that way."

She shook her head. "No. Not at all," she said quietly.

He was silent. "It's funny, really—looking back. I don't know if you've ever lived with someone"—she shook her head—"Well, at the beginning, it's heaven on earth. You're in heaven when you're together, nearly in pain when you're apart." He frowned. "I'm surprised that you haven't been married. Or at least lived with someone."

She shrugged, suddenly self-conscious. "I—it just hasn't happened." She smiled ironically. "I tend to have rather misguided taste in men, I'm afraid—present company excepted."

"What about your folks?" he asked. "Are they still together?"

She quickly shook her head. "No. My, uh, father left us when I was five, and my mother's been remarried—let's see, twice. The second time was last year."

"That must have been very hard for you—when you were young, I mean."

"Oh, well," she said, trying to shrug it off. "It's all over now."

His eyes were serious. "You're very important to me, Kate." He paused. "Over the past couple of nights I've thought about some of the things I've said to you, and some of the things I've done—and if I've seemed too forward or too confident or smooth, it's only because I've been confident of you—that you're very, very right for me."

He set his drink down, then reached forward and took hers out of her hand. She looked into his eyes, knowing this was the moment, this was what she had wanted, and also, at some level, feared. She wanted him—wanted to believe what he said about her, wanted to believe that she could love him, wanted all of it to work out—as it never had before. Yet the moment was so familiar, so reminiscent. This moment—before a kiss, an embrace, a touch that would lead to fulfillment of desire—she had experienced before. With the same fluttery anticipation, the same hope, the same need. She knew it well. And she hoped that somehow, Ben would be different, that this moment would lead to something more than she had ever had.

"Kate," he said softly.

Her gaze slid back to his.

"Tell me," he murmured, leaning forward so his lips were only inches from hers. "Tell me what you want," he whispered, brushing his lips against hers. The movement triggered a rush of desire, and the feel of his rough cheek against hers made her wind her arms around him, feeling for the strength of his shoulders, the softness of his hair.

"I know what you meant," he breathed, moving a hand on to her thigh. "I know what you meant about spontaneity, about being unpremeditated and completely free." His hand moved upward, kneading her flesh with persuasive fingers. "But, Kate, you have to tell me if you want me, if the time is right or wrong or bad or good. Because every time I'm with you, I'm thinking of our making love." Her hands moved over his shoulders and downward, roving across his chest, finding his hardened nipples beneath the fabric of his shirt. "I imagine my lips awakening you," he breathed, nibbling at her ear, "and my touch arousing you," he murmured, his hand moving between her thighs.

"Ben," she whispered, melting against him.

She sank back, looking up at him as he gazed down at her with smoldering pleasure, his fingers sending surges of molten yearning through her.

She reached out, wanting to feel the strength she craved, wanting to bring him the pleasure he was giving her.

But he sat back and murmured, "Not yet," as she whispered his name.

"I've thought of you so often," he said softly, "of this moment, of seeing how beautiful you are." And his hands moved downward then, along her thighs and then up to the buttons of her dress.

As they parted the fabric and exposed her small, high breasts, he inhaled sharply. He knelt over her then, awakening each nipple with a long, warm kiss, sending a flush of desire through her whole body. His lips brought each nipple to a tingling peak, and then he gently nibbled, sending sparks of flame through her body and soul.

She quivered, as he rose and trailed his hands down over her stomach and hips, in lazy, tantalizing circles. The touch of his fingers was light but incredibly arousing, sweeping from her thighs over her hips, across her stomach, over the softness they had brought to a pitch of trembling want, and Kate arched under his touch.

She reached out for him then, but again he whispered, "Not yet." And deftly he slid the silk of her dress from her body, pulled the lace bikinis from her hips and off, and she lay naked under his smoldering gaze. "Oh, Kate," he murmured, and slowly, achingly slowly, he began a lazy, fervid exploration of her body, lowering himself and melting her with pleasure in the touch of his fingers and the warm tip of his tongue.

She was lost in dizzying rapture as his hands played

over the softness of her breasts and their sensitized peaks, as his wet lips roved across her stomach. He kneaded her nipples between his fingers until she whispered his name, then slid his hands lower, over her hips to her thighs. And then he began a flaming onslaught of pleasure as he moved lower, his fingers coaxing the sensitive skin of her inner thighs, his tongue gently exploring with a delicacy that made her tremble.

She reached for him, clutching at his hair with her fingers, writhing beneath him in the ever-growing glow of passion.

"Ben, take me." She needed him with her, deeply and with a passion that was all-encompassing.

And he rose then, looking at her with deep amber eyes heavy with desire. He began unbuttoning his shirt, never taking his eyes from Kate, and she rose up to help him, pulling off his shirt, unfastening his belt, fingers quick in the heat of the moment.

His body was magnificent standing before her—lean, strong, ready. Then he lay beside her, moved warm hungry hands back to the place that had given her so much fiery pleasure, and she clutched at him, raking her hands along his firm back, moaning into his neck. "Ben, take me," she whispered.

As he shifted, fitting his beautiful body over hers, she looked into his eyes and saw love—deep, giving, shining down into her eyes with the brightness of stars.

"I've wanted this so much," he said breathlessly. And he brought them together in one magnificent movement, crying out her name as she melted into him. The rhythm of their love was fast, deep, rolling, punctuated with sighs of pleasure, moans of need, whispered words of love. She loved the feel of his back, wet and strong under her fingers, the scent of his maleness, the feel of his chest against hers as he stoked the fires within her with masterly flaming thrusts. And then Kate was aware of nothing but the deepest of surging pleasures, rapture that brought her together with Ben in a bliss that dissolved all but sensation, all but a feeling that they were a perfect oneness.

And then slowly, gradually, she was aware of an awakening love that would grow, she was sure now, deeper than any she had ever known.

Never had she felt so wonderful—so thoroughly happy, relaxed, free. She felt weightless, free of all cares, all worries, everything but the moment. As she and Ben shifted, her cheek against his warm, strong chest, arms and legs entwined with his, she knew that she had finally come to know what she cared for so deeply in him. She had found his core, the essence of his being: it was his strength, the self-knowledge that was so strong and so deep that it allowed him to give as no other man could give.

"Darling," he murmured, wrapping his warm arms more tightly around her. He moved so he could look into her eyes.

She smiled happily into his. "I'm so glad," she said quietly.

"I wonder if you're as happy as I am," he mused. His hands stroked the curves of her body, the rise of her hips and the valley of her waist, and she loved his touch now more than ever. "It's been a very, very long time since I've felt anything close to what I feel now," he said quietly.

"Have you—has it been a long time since you've been involved with anyone? I don't even know." She hesitated. "There's so much about you I don't know." In a sense she felt that was no longer true; for in their lovemaking he had given of himself, shown himself, as no other man had. But there were still questions. . . .

"I haven't been involved with anyone in quite a while," he said. "Let's see—nearly a year now. I've gone out here and there with women I already knew, and a few I'd just met, but I haven't been serious . . . and in the past year, I've always broken off the relationships early on."

He turned on his side and faced her, putting a warm thigh between her own and a hand at her waist. She loved looking into his eyes as he talked. They looked deeper somehow, as if she hadn't truly realized their beauty until now.

"I guess I made a decision," he said quietly, "a couple of years ago, when I was almost forty and kind cf taking stock of my life, looking at what I had done and what I hoped to do. I was happy about some things—pleased with my work, though not satisfied, but I felt I had achieved some measure of success. And pleased that I had married, that I had had something to do with raising two great kids. But I knew I was ready for more." He paused, gently caressing the soft skin of her waist. "I don't think of my first marriage as a failure. Celia and I were very, very happy at the beginning. And we had Eliza and Christopher. But I want to try again. I've had kids; I don't need to have more. But I do want a partner again, a woman I can share my life with. There are a lot of men out there who are afraid of commitment, Kate. Maybe like your friend Kurt. But I'm not one of them." He sighed. "I've had some awful moments over the last couple of years, when I've broken off relationships because I knew there was no potential. And obviously, it's gone both ways, with women I really liked who thought the relationship couldn't go any farther." He smiled. "Anyway, that's a very long answer to your question, Kate, but it's the best one I can give."

She smiled. "Those women who broke up with you were fools." She reached up and pushed a dark lock of hair back from his forehead.

He laughed. "Thanks for the vote of confidence. But they seemed very, very sure of what they were doing."

"Well they were crazy," she said, cuddling her leg over his and resting her cheek on his shoulder. She loved looking up into his eyes like this, holding him so close, talking so quietly.

Such a contrast, too, to those times with Kurt and others, when there was silence after lovemaking, or almost worse, forced conversation, as if they thought they were "doing the right thing" by saying how wonderful it was, using stock phrases out of magazines and movies.

As Kate began to fall into a dreamy half-sleep, lulled by the comforting rhythm of Ben's breathing and the warmth of his arms around her, she felt her carefree sense of security and happiness begin to ebb away. Gradually, as Ben fell asleep, Kate grew more and more awake, her eyes wide open against the smooth skin of his shoulder.

It had been too good. She couldn't shake the feeling, couldn't suppress the growing voice from somewhere deep inside that said, *Don't fall for this. Don't be so blind. He's much too good to be true.*

She shut her eyes, trying to think. What had he said? That he wanted to be serious; that he was ready for a relationship; that he wasn't afraid. He hadn't said any of those things about her, but he didn't have to; the implication was clear. Wasn't it?

She tried to remember more. He had said he had broken up with women he had been involved with, when he had seen that there was no potential in the relationship. Had that been a warning of sorts, a statement that the same could happen with her? And when she had said she thought the women who had broken up with him were crazy to have done so, had she gone too far?

Her heart quickened as she tried to think of the answers. And she cursed herself for having driven the beautiful feeling of peace she had had from her mind. Ben was lying entwined with her, sleeping, dreaming already, and she was racking her brain for answers she couldn't possibly know.

She supposed it was the legacy of the life she had led, a lifetime of wrong decisions and misguided choices. And she silently cursed the men she had been involved with, too. She knew her once-burned twice-shy attitude wasn't their fault, but she couldn't help resenting them anyway. For she desperately wanted her relationship with Ben to last—at least for a while. And she couldn't help feeling, deep down, that there wasn't a chance in the world that this could possibly happen. At some point, very soon or in the near future, he would turn out to be like the others.

CHAPTER SIX

Kate's worries drifted away as she drifted off into sleep. And with sleep came a peace she desperately needed. In her dreams she made love with Ben, and he told her he loved her as he had never loved before. But then the dream turned into a nightmare: Kate opened her mouth to tell Ben she loved him, but when she tried, no words came. Only silence.

She awakened, shaken by the dream, by having been unable to express herself. Yet, as she looked at Ben—slowly awakening, eyes opening and lighting up as they looked into hers—she knew that, as in the dream, she could say nothing; words would be too dangerous, too much a courting of rejection or silence. And she was certain, also, that she saw love in Ben's eyes, felt it in every loving touch, every whispered word of lovemaking. And for now that would have to be enough.

He sighed against her cheek and smiled. "Sorry," he whispered.

"For what?"

He raised a sleepy brow and smiled. "Isn't falling asleep after lovemaking considered a big faux pas these days in women's magazines?"

She laughed. "Women's magazines? Do I look like a magazine? Quit trying to be perfect. Anyway, they're talking about something different when they write about that—the guy who rolls off you like a log, grunts, turns over, and starts snoring half a second later. You hardly fit into that category."

He smiled. "I'm glad of that. Did you sleep?"

She nodded against his shoulder.

"Nice dreams?" he asked.

"Mm," she lied, wishing he hadn't asked.

"Can you stay the night?" he murmured, a hand silkily roving over her hips, along a thigh. Kate's body responded quickly to his touch, knowing the pitch of fevered arousal it could bring her to.

She was instantly awash with desire, possessed by a throbbing inner need that was his and his alone to satisfy.

"Hm?" he asked, his warm hand asking its own question as it moved to the satin of her inner thighs.

"I don't know," she whispered breathlessly, teasingly, as she reached out for him.

His hand caught her wrist and he looked into her eyes with a penetrating gaze of challenge. "Hm? What are you up to, then?"

With his other hand he grasped the softness between her thighs, making her whisper his name.

"You'll stay, then," he rasped.

"Yes. Oh, yes."

He released her hand and she reached out for him, her fingers trailing in hungry exploration from his rippling chest down to his slim hips. They worked downward, needing to stroke those parts of him she loved to look at—his long, muscular thighs, the lean edges of his hips.

And then she reached for him, wanting to bring him the same melting pleasure he was bringing her.

"My God, woman," he whispered, trembling under her loving touch, "what you do to me."

"I want you," she said, her words muffled, fired by the strength of his response to her touch.

"Come to me again," he urged. "I need you."

And as he moved on top of her and merged her burning want with his in a powerful thrust of love, she cried out his name with passion.

He felt like blazing pleasure inside her, stroking rapture that transported her with him to spiraling heights. They climbed together, grasping, urging, whispering, coaxing, fusing, a trembling mixture of exquisite delight and urgency, bliss and arousal. And they flamed in a shimmering coursing ecstasy that lost them both, for a time, to everything but feeling, and then afterward, gently rolling, slowing, winding down, to the deepest of love and wonder at each other.

"Kate," he whispered, nuzzling his lips against her ear. "You're so beautiful. So wonderful. I—I love you."

Her heart soared. "I love you, too, Ben," she said, holding him tight. "I love you, too."

Kate stayed the night, sleeping half the time and making love the other half, and her fears flew out of her heart as she grew to trust Ben more and more deeply, to give of herself more freely each time they embraced.

She rose in the pale-gray light of dawn, getting dressed as Ben slept. She loved the way the light coming across the East River had awakened her; it was so different from her own dark apartment. And the view from Ben's window—indeed, from the bed—was among the most tranquil she had ever seen. The city, the river, and Long Island City beyond were asleep, still and dark against the long rays of the rising sun.

"You're not leaving," came his voice from behind her.

She turned and smiled. "I have to. I have an early meeting today."

He sighed. "But I'll see you at two for our meeting at the agency."

She nodded. "And I have to talk to you about something that happened."

He sat up against the bed frame. "What? Tell me now, if it's important."

She hesitated. The night—and the early morning—had been so wonderful; she didn't want to cloud its rosiness by bringing up business—especially something unpleasant like Dick Dayton.

"What is it?" he pressed.

She sighed and went over to the bed and sat at its edge. "Oh, Ben, it's nothing that major. But I hate discussing something like business with you after—after last night."

He smiled. "We're going to have to sometime," he said, taking her hand. "And it doesn't undo anything, you know."

She smiled. "I guess you're right." And she told him about her conversation with Dayton and his very strong suggestion that they use his niece for the campaign.

Ben shook his head when she was finished. "That man is a fool," he said quietly.

"He's a fool," Kate said, "but more than that, Ben, he can't be trusted. As far as I'm concerned, that conversation sealed Alexandra's fate. I can't possibly hire her."

Ben drew his head back. "What?"

"I'm sorry, Ben. But if Dayton is interfering this much now, imagine what he'll do later. He'll probably dictate the *clothes* she's going to wear, for God's sake."

Ben was expressionless, his voice flat as he said, "So you're going to let a great model go because of an uncle you don't think you can handle."

Kate's lips tightened. "Maybe I can handle him, Ben. And maybe I can't. The point is that I think it's courting disaster to walk into a situation like that knowing what the possibilities are. There are other models. Other actresses."

"Dammit, Kate, listen to me. Don't make this mistake. I promise you—when you've been in the business as long as I have, you'll know: you can't expect to find another Alexandra Dayton. Not easily. Don't mess this one up, Kate. Just believe me. This is the type of situation you'll have to learn to deal with, that's all."

She looked at him, at the amber eyes she couldn't read, the hard set of his mouth. What she had feared was already beginning to happen: the warmth, the love that had touched them both suddenly seemed a memory. "I don't want to talk about it anymore," she said, turning away.

"Why not?" he demanded. "Kate, I want to see you do the best damned job anyone's ever done on a campaign at Ivorsen and Shaw. And that means you've got to let me help you. And you've got to take some risks you might be afraid to take."

"Why do you assume I'm afraid, Ben? Why don't you see it as reasonable caution?" She sighed. "Anyway, I just—I'm not sure how to say this." His eyes gave her no encouragement, but she went on. "I—it makes me uncomfortable to hear you talk in such a controlling way about me. In any other area, maybe I wouldn't mind. But with my work—with *our* work—it makes me feel as if you're trying to mold me into something—to make me into something I'm not."

"I'm trying to make you as good as you can be."

"Then let me make my own mistakes," she said. "And learn that way."

He shook his head with a certainty that surprised her. "I can't do that," he said. "You have to trust me, Kate. That's all I can say."

They batted the issue of Alexandra Dayton around for the next half hour—with Kate resisting, Ben pushing calmly but logically. And Kate finally agreed: it did make more sense to hire Alexandra Dayton and prepare to deal with difficulties with her uncle than to lose her altogether. And Kate did feel—whatever Ben thought—that she was strong enough to handle Dick Dayton.

Later in the day, when Kate saw Ben at his office for the second round of auditions, she didn't feel any of the controlling dominance she had minded earlier. The audition went well, too—exceptionally well, according to Ben and Andrew Coates—and afterward, in a meeting, they all agreed that Alexandra Dayton would be the new I and S woman, and a young man who had just auditioned, Pierce Allen, would be the new I and S man. Pierce was a perfect complement to Alexandra, with thick, dark hair, pale blue eyes, fine, small features, and a tall, lean frame. He was twenty-five to her twenty-one, and though he was, in a sense, more classically good-looking than she, he was her perfect partner; together, they were sure to catch everyone's attention. And the two had a wonderful rapport together, both in the audition and afterward on videotape. Kate was thrilled.

Over the next few days Ben's team of copywriters worked around the clock honing and polishing the copy for the upcoming print ads and the scripts for the upcoming TV and radio ads. Kate met daily with Ben, Alexandra, and Pierce at the Blake-Canfield offices, and she spent every afternoon with Alexandra and Pierce as well, planning their wardrobes, accessories, and sets with Blake-Canfield's stylist.

During this time Kate tried to keep her mind on her work and off her relationship with Ben. He was just as affectionate as before, and certainly demonstrative, even in the office: giving her quick kisses when they were alone, looking at her with eyes clearly full of desire and need. Yet, at the end of each morning session, as Kate was getting ready to return to Ivorsen and Shaw, Ben never made any specific overture. He would say only that he would see her the next day and set the time for the appointment.

At first Kate took his words at face value; he was, after all, definitely still romantic, still assuming they would be together soon. But then she began to wonder; perhaps he was trying to ease out of the relationship, letting it slip away as if it had never existed.

And she was suddenly frightened, with a swiftness that came from having lived through this so many times before. He had said he loved her; she had said she loved him. He had told her of his desire for a serious relationship. And of the way he eased out of relationships with no potential. And perhaps, she thought, he was easing out of this one.

Finally, on the day the shooting of the first print ads was scheduled to begin, Kate knew she would have to speak with Ben about her concerns. She simply couldn't go on any longer, not knowing, not saying anything. Breaking up with Kurt had been her first step on a path of what she had hoped would be a new course of maturity: not standing for nonsense, not falling for lines, not lying down for any kind of emotional game-playing. And if she was going to stick to her resolves, it was definitely time to act. But she found, when Ben arrived at I and S that evening for the shooting, that there was no time to talk. Naturally, the place was in chaos, with the furniture department, where the shooting was to take place, resembling a movie set more than a store.

When Ben had first arrived, he had spoken briefly to Kate about the shooting, but he was now off talking with his stylist and art director. And Kate, in any case, had other problems to worry about for the moment: Alexandra Dayton had been shaky and nervous all afternoon; Dick Dayton, who had been remarkably quiet since Alexandra had been hired, was now eating antacids by the handful and almost constantly haranguing Kate; and Kurt, on the scene in his capacity as I and S acting art director, was bothering Kate by his presence alone.

As the time for the shooting drew near, Kate went over to help the stylist get Alexandra and Pierce ready for the first ad. Set in a large room, empty except for a giant brass bed and a one-of-a-kind antique brass lamp, the ad was designed to show stark but utter luxury. Alexandra would be dressed in a peach-satin teddy and Pierce in black silk pajama-bottoms. Each would be half-covered by an antique patchwork quilt that would be draped on the bed in various strategic positions.

Panic broke loose when Kate discovered that the peach teddy hardly showed in the test Polaroids, making Alexandra look very close to nude. But the peach teddy was exchanged for a black one—"much sexier anyway," Ben said, eliciting a dark look from Kate—and the shooting finally began.

Kate loved the concept of the ad. It was going to be a full page, run in all the major newspapers, and as Kate watched the shooting, she could just feel it would be a success. The photographer, a young, graceful man dressed all in black, had Alexandra and Pierce try all variations of expression and movement. Alexandra managed to swing through a whole spectrum of moods—at one moment kitten-cuddly, at the next sleek and seductive, all answers to Pierce's different poses and expressions. Finally, the shooting for the first ad ended.

Shooting on the second one, set in the store's luxurious lingerie department, went a bit more smoothly. The ad was one of Kate's favorites, with Pierce looking at Alexandra—dressed in the black teddy from the first ad—holding a handful of lingerie and posing very suggestively.

Alexandra was once again uninhibited about the shot. She was a different animal in front of the lens of a camera, as confident there as she was shy on her own. Dick Dayton, on the other hand, nearly had to be restrained when he saw what his niece was wearing. Kate, silently telling herself she had known this would happen—and giving Ben a look that said, "I told you so"—went over to Dayton and quietly but firmly calmed him down. With the very clear suggestion ringing in his ears that he was actually interfering with his niece's potential future success, he retreated into the back of the crowd, and finally the lingerie shots were completed.

The rest—in the sporting-goods, men's-wear, and resort-wear departments—went quickly. After more than three hours of shooting, the crew and cast were getting a bit punchy—laughing at the slightest mistake, collapsing into helpless giggling fits every few minutes; but just as Kate was beginning to worry, Ben leaned over to her and whispered, "Beautiful. We couldn't have asked for better." And Kate realized he was right: the happiness and sheer delight that shone from both Alexandra's and Pierce's eyes would do more for the ads than anything else the agency could possibly have come up with.

And then, finally, the shooting was over. Makeup, props, clothes, were packed up, cameras and backdrops rolled away, lights removed.

Alexandra, looking dazed and happy, came over to Kate and thanked her, and was joined moments later by her uncle. "I think we can all agree that everyone did a wonderful job," he said, putting his arms around Alexandra and Kate. "Just wonderful."

Kate forced a smile, but was saved from further pretense when Alexandra suddenly excused herself and went running off toward the elevator. The sight distracted both Kate and Dayton, who watched silently as Alexandra stopped Kurt with a gentle hand on his elbow. Kate saw a smile on Kurt's face—a slow, familiar-looking smile she recognized as the one he used when recognizing that he had been "chosen" again.

Kate turned back to Dick Dayton, still at her side, and was surprised—and taken aback—to see the look of fury in his eyes as he watched his niece talking with Kurt.

Then he turned to Kate. "What do you know about that Kurt Reeves?" he demanded.

"He's a very good art director," she said truthfully.

"What else?" he barked.

"What is it that you want to know?" she asked calmly.

He looked at her for a moment, and then sighed. "Never mind," he muttered. "I'll find out for myself." And he stalked off in the direction of Alexandra and Kurt.

A moment later Ben was at Kate's side. She smiled up at him. "You just missed an interesting little exchange," she said. "It seems Dick Dayton has a new object of suspicion and mistrust."

Ben looked over at Dayton. "Kurt?"

Kate nodded. "Who seems to have found a new object as well."

Ben raised a brow. "She does seem rather interested, doesn't she?"

"Well, he knows how to use his not inconsiderable charm when he has to." She paused. "Do you think he's good-looking, Ben?"

Ben smiled. "A loaded question if I ever heard one." He looked over at Kurt, and Kate followed his gaze. "Yes, I'd have to say he was—except there's something very . . . very manipulative in his manner. I don't think Stan, our AD, is too happy about working with him."

"Well, who knows? Maybe he'll be on his best behavior now that he's set his sights on our new Miss I and S. I recognize all the signs."

Ben gave her an odd, unreadable look. "Jealous?"

"No, of course not!" She looked into his eyes, trying to fathom his thoughts, wondering if now was the right time to talk. They were alone except for a few crew members packing up. Dayton, Alexandra, and Kurt had gone off, and the area was quiet, calm once again.

"But I do have to talk to you," she said quietly.

He frowned. "What's the matter? You look upset."

"Well, I don't know," she said tentatively, wondering whether she hadn't in fact been overanalyzing. But she had to tell him how she felt. "It's just that I'm not quite sure what's going on with us. We've both been so busy that—I'm just not sure where we're heading."

"I *have* been busy," he said. "I've been on the verge of neglecting my other clients, Kate. But to tell you the truth, I haven't wanted to push anything. It's—if something is right, it will happen on its own."

So he was uncertain, then. Hesitant and uncertain. "I see," she said quietly.

"Do you?" he asked.

"I think so," she said hollowly, forcing out the words. "And I suppose you're right, really, when you think about it. Well," she said, "it's late, and I'm tired, so I guess I'll be getting home."

"I'll take you," he said.

She shook her head. "That's all right. I can get a cab."

For a moment they looked into each other's eyes, each trying to read the other's thoughts. "I'll walk you out, then," he said.

In the elevator, when Kate looked at Ben, his eyes were opaque, distant. "I think you'll be very pleased with the prints, Kate. Do you want me to send them over tomorrow or do you want to come by?"

"When will they be ready?" she asked, aware only that she was speaking words that seemed to make sense. But her heart was still trying to unravel what had happened.

"Uh, tomorrow morning by nine or ten, I imagine. The paste-up assistants will work with the prints I think are best, but I'll send the whole batch over to you. Then all we need is client approval before they go in to the papers."

Kate stared. *Client approval,* she thought. Wasn't it all getting rather impersonal? She sighed. "Well. Send them to my office," she said. "Kurt and some other people will want to see them."

"Right," he said quietly, and they left the elevator and walked through the ground floor, now nearly dark, empty except for a lone cleaning woman at the far end of the floor.

The night watchman came out from a utility room and opened the door for them, and they stepped out into the chill of the night air.

"Well, good night," Ben said.

"Good night," she said quietly.

He leaned down and kissed her on the mouth. But when she opened her eyes, they were met by his questioning gaze.

"Good night," he said again, pulling back and straightening. And he turned and walked off into the night.

CHAPTER SEVEN

During the taxi ride home, Kate stared straight ahead, seeing nothing, hearing nothing, trying to block out the distant look she remembered in Ben's eyes. She tried to make her mind blank, to think of something else. But all she could remember was Ben, his quiet voice saying, "If something is right, it will happen on its own." And she tried to close her eyes against a flood of bitter tears.

She had been so sure. Not sure that he had been perfect, or wonderful in every way. But she had been sure he was a man who took relationships—and lovemaking—seriously. And she had been certain, above all else, that the relationship would be more than a brief one, more than a quick fling.

Once in her apartment, Kate kicked off her shoes, flicked on the TV, and threw herself on the living room couch. She knew sleep would be impossible, and lying in the darkness by herself would be unbearably lonely. She missed Ben. She wanted him. And what she had loved about him most—a security that seemed to imply commitment, seriousness, respect for other people's feelings—had turned out to be an illusion and nothing more.

She tried to fix her gaze on the television screen. A man

had a woman in his arms; rain was streaking the windows behind them; flames were leaping in the fireplace to their side. And as the man lowered his head to the woman's lips, he whispered, "I love you. And I'm home, darling. Home for good." As their lips met, violins sang of their love.

Kate picked up a paperback and threw it at the screen. The movie looked like it had been terrible—one corny line after another. Yet even so, it had reached her, bringing tears to her eyes. For even in the worst of scripts, love—a love she craved, a love she had hoped for—came through.

The ringing of the downstairs buzzer brought Kate out of her thoughts. She looked at her watch—it was nearly quarter to one! She padded over to the intercom that connected with the doorman's office in the lobby. "Yes?"

"A Mr. Austin is here, Miss Churchill."

She bit her lip. Now what? "Please send him up, Fred. Thanks."

Kate raced out of the foyer and into the bathroom to see whether she looked as terrible as she felt. Her eye makeup was smudged and her lashes were caked together, but she managed to dab away most of the black and was left with slightly too-dark eyes and very pale-looking skin.

But as she left the bathroom and went back into the living room, she angrily observed to herself that her eyes were not, really, the problem. Far more worrisome was whether she would be able to deal with Ben as she wanted to. And as she heard the sound of the elevator down the hall, she realized she didn't even know what it was she wanted to say or do.

The doorbell rang, and she answered it quickly, opening the door and backing up to let Ben in without even looking at him.

He came inside quickly, but stayed in the foyer rather than going on into the living room.

She looked up at him, anger mixing with uncertainty. "I didn't expect to see you—obviously."

He sighed, sadness in his eyes. "I had to come," he said. "And I had to see you, to talk to you face to face. Can we sit down?"

She walked ahead of him to the living room, still unsure of her feelings.

A few moments later Ben, on the couch beside her, was looking into her eyes. "I lied to you back at the store," he said.

Kate blinked, trying to hold in the pit of fear that was growing in her stomach. He had lied. About what? Was he seeing someone else? Was it completely over between them? "Go on," she said quietly.

He reached into his pocket and took out his pipe and tobacco. For the first time it was a gesture that annoyed Kate. "Hey," she said. "Can't that wait? You just said something I'd like to hear the rest of."

He smiled. "You're right. Sorry. All right, this is it. I've been trying—in various ways and at various times—to stay away from you, to keep what's happening between us at some sort of reasonable level." Listening, she felt the warmth of relaxation begin to flow through her again, and she realized she had been holding her breath. "I remember you at the beginning, when we first met—very cautious, very wary, asking me to back up and back off." He smiled. "And then it all changed, very much as I wanted it to."

She looked into his eyes. "And it's too much?"

He shook his head. "Not for me—not at all. But Kate,

how long has it been since you broke up with that Reeves fellow?"

She shrugged. "I don't know, exactly. Not very long. But so what?"

" 'So what' is that you've spent your life—according to what you've told me—holding off from commitments, staying closed off from whatever man you're involved with."

She lifted her chin. "And?"

"And I don't know that you're ready. . . . I don't want to rush into something that gets ruined because you happen to be on the rebound."

She stared at him. "I—you don't think I'm 'ready'?"

"Are you?"

"Ben, how can you *presume* like that? I can't believe you're making that kind of assumption."

"I have because I've been listening to you, Kate. You worry—or used to worry—about double signals. You're very aware of a look you might give me, or a touch, or a suggestion through your tone of voice. But maybe you've forgotten some of the things you've actually said to me in words, Kate. And they're things I've taken to heart. I want to keep seeing you, dammit—and not have you running scared."

"Do you call the other night 'running scared' when we made love at your house?"

"Of course not," he said quietly.

"Then why don't you let me be the judge of my feelings, Ben? And trust me that much. God, how can you even want me if you think I'm unsure?"

"Don't ever doubt that I want you. Not ever," he murmured, reaching out and touching the cool skin of her neck.

"Then, dammit," she said quietly, "stop doubting *me.*" Her eyes met his in a gaze of sudden, burning acknowledgment of what they shared, of what they knew of each other's passions and needs and desires. "Oh, Ben," she whispered, just before his lips claimed hers in a torrid kiss.

They undressed quickly, lovingly, each lingering and then making up for lost time—he cupping her breasts in warm hands, kneading each nipple until Kate moaned with pleasure against his neck, she lingering as she edged off his pants tantalizingly slowly, running her fingers over his hard thighs with heated persuasion.

When they lay beside each other, warm skin against warm skin, Kate planted her lips against his neck and then began roving them downward, letting them follow a trail already seared by her fingers. "You see," she murmured into the soft hairs of his chest, "you shouldn't doubt me when you know how much pleasure you give me, when you know how I can feel free with you as I haven't ever before."

She took a nipple between her teeth and gently tugged at it. Ben moaned, pulling her closer, his hands holding her by the shoulders.

She let her hands trail lower, down the firm ripples of his chest to the line of hair at its center as she continued her tantalizing tugging at his nipples. And then she followed the path of her hands, down the fine line of dark hair. Ben's hands were in her hair, caressing it with need.

"Touch me," he whispered, kneading her, moving beneath her.

And she watched with pleasure as he trembled beneath the touch of her fingers, pulsated into arousal with thrilling strength. She melted at the sight of his ardor and lowered her lips, wanting to give him the surging pleasure he had given her. She thrilled to the pleasure of his desire, shifted at his urging, let his fingers explore and rediscover her with the urgency of the moment. He coaxed as she kissed, whispered as she moaned, let his hands work magic until she was burning.

And then they came together with thrilling force, fiery thrusts that sent them into a spiraling glow of heated pleasure. Their flames grew, surged, blazed, finally bursting into a shuddering release and melting pleasure that was everything.

"Darling," Ben whispered as he lay, spent, in her arms. "Promise you won't ever doubt my love for you."

She smiled. "I promise," she whispered back. And she happily fell asleep, her cheek against his chest, her breathing in tune with his.

The next morning Kate awakened as Ben was leaning over, kissing her softly on one eyelid and then the other.

She smiled, stretched lazily and contentedly, and pulled Ben down on top of her.

"Mm," he said, and kissed her gently and then more deeply.

"Darling." When he pulled away, his hazel eyes were dark with desire. "This morning is going to be a great exercise in self-control," he said, pulling back on to his knees.

She smiled up at him. "Oh, really?" she asked, letting

her fingers trail along the hardness of his thighs. "I had thought you could stay."

He shook his head, a smile just beneath the look of seriousness. "Can't do."

"Are you sure?" she asked, sitting up. She saw the pleasure in his eyes as he looked at her breasts, felt the desire she knew she could kindle. "I had just thought," she said, moving forward, "that there was some kind of allowance in your schedule for a little morning pleasure."

She could see his breathing coming faster, and she leaned forward and took a nipple between her teeth. He moaned and cupped her breasts in his warm hands, then pulled her up for a deep kiss.

He tore his mouth from hers. "I really do have to leave," he said hoarsely.

"Then go ahead," she said, leaning forward and catching his warm thighs in her hands. "Just go ahead."

His desire rose as she moved her hands upward and let her fingers work their magic. "If you want to," she breathed, "then go."

And she looked into his eyes with challenge that was instantly replaced with desire.

"I want you," he said, and he took her again, with a coursing, stroking, masterful passion that was deep and quick and utterly rapturous.

"You are a temptress and a seductress and a manipulator, Kate Churchill," he said into the curve of her neck.

She smiled lazily. "I've been known to get what I want on occasion."

He turned and studied her eyes. "And do you have what you want?" he asked quietly.

She smiled hesitantly, suddenly uncomfortable. "I had a wonderful night, and a wonderful morning."

He looked at her and said nothing. And then she remembered the dream in which she had been unable to tell Ben she loved him; and she realized she was still frightened to give herself completely, to show herself and all her feelings.

At Ivorsen and Shaw that morning photostats of the sample layouts, along with proofs of all the shots from the photo session, arrived on Kate's desk at ten o'clock on the dot. They looked wonderful, and Ben had selected the very best of the shots to be included in the actual layouts. She called his office to tell him how much she liked the ads, and that they would almost certainly be approved and ready to go right away. But Ben was out, and she simply left a message.

And then she geared herself up to go see Kurt and Dick Dayton. Kurt, as acting art director, was the only other person who had to okay the layouts formally. But Kate knew that her predecessor had always informally "run them past Dick," as he used to say, and Kate's intuition told her it would be wise to follow the usual procedure.

As it turned out, Dick Dayton loved the ads. He had apparently learned a lesson at the shooting about interfering, and he was very quiet, even respectful of Kate as she showed him the layouts.

Kate left Dayton's office with a glow of confidence she hoped would last with Kurt as well. When she walked into his office, he was on the phone, and she was glad—though she didn't exactly know why—that she was the one who saw him first rather than the other way around. Perhaps it had something to do with Dick Dayton's favorite game —power—but she wasn't altogether sure. In any case Kurt looked up almost immediately, quick as a cat, and then swiveled his chair so his back was to Kate.

He's gearing himself up, she thought as she brought the layouts over to his drafting table by the window. *But I'm ready for him.*

She looked around at the office she knew so well, marveling at how different it all looked now that her relationship with Kurt was over. On his desk the picture of himself that had once intrigued her now pointed up his immaturity; the low-volume but very noticeable rock music pulsating from the stereo behind Kurt's desk was more annoying than relaxing; and Kurt himself—chuckling softly into the receiver, with his legs up on the windowsill and his head flung back in an attitude of feigned nonchalance was, of course, the most disturbing of all. For Kate could hardly bear to think she had once—very recently—been involved with this young man, and that she might even have missed the chance to be with Ben had she been more deeply involved with Kurt. The thought sent a chill through her.

Finally, Kurt hung up and turned to Kate with an expectant and confident look.

"I'm here with the layouts," she said flatly, in a tone which very clearly suggested this was obvious.

But he didn't seem to notice. *Too self-absorbed,* she realized as she watched him come over to the drafting table where she stood. For in his near swagger of a walk, he showed he was still interested—if not in her, then in her interest, in attraction for attraction's sake.

Kate talked as quickly as she could, flipping through

the layouts and then looking into Kurt's eyes as she finished. "The first, as you know, is scheduled for insertion the day after tomorrow, so obviously all the approvals have to be given now. This morning, actually."

" 'All' the approvals? Yours, mine, and who else's?"

Her lips tightened. "Just yours and mine, actually."

He smiled sarcastically. "Ah. Together again," he said, turning back to the layouts. He was looking closely—very closely—at the layout for the first ad. "Hm. Sloppy work," he said quietly.

Her stomach jumped. "What?"

He waved a hand. "Sloppy work. Look at that makeup. Makes Alexandra look like a tramp."

Kate took a deep breath, readying herself. Then she turned to Kurt and looked him squarely in his once-pretty blue eyes. "Stop right there," she said, her voice harsh. "I know what you're doing, and it's silly and childish and very, very annoying."

He cocked his head and looked at her seriously. "What are you talking about?"

"I'm talking about your obvious search for flaws, Kurt. And your obvious plan to withhold or at least delay approval."

He smiled. "Is that what you think?" Then his eyes grew serious. "Rather self-centered of you, I think. I plan, yes, to look these over very carefully. But only because I want to be certain Alexandra looks her very, very best."

"Ah," Kate said quietly. "How nice. And generous, too."

Kurt picked up one of the layouts and ran a finger along Alexandra's picture. "I'm her rep as of last night, Kate. You'll be dealing with me now in her negotiations."

Kate raised a brow. "*I* won't be dealing with you or anyone else, Kurt—that's handled by Blake-Canfield. But let's get this straight: you were *not* her rep, nor her agent, nor her anything else when these pictures were taken. She does not have the right of approval in her contract. Whatever you have to say about these layouts, you say in your capacity as acting art director for I and S. Now, I plan to send these stats back, with my okay *and* your okay on them, by no later than eleven o'clock this morning. And, Kurt, if your approval *isn't* on these layouts, don't expect Miss Alexandra Dayton to get any work from Ivorsen and Shaw *or* Blake-Canfield again." She met the glittering look of shock and anger in his eyes with as cool a look of determination as she could muster.

"I'll get back to you," he said quietly.

And, knowing that was Kurt's only graceful way of acceding, she left his office. An hour later the stats were on her desk, marked OK KR.

Kate was pleased, but she knew that he would find some way, somehow, to get back at her. Not for having ended the relationship—he had been asking for that; indeed, he seemed to have found someone else as quickly as she had. No, he had shown his feelings for her very clearly in that last, unpleasant phone call. But she suspected that he couldn't forgive her for going on so easily without him.

The thought worried her. And what bothered her most about it was that she felt she couldn't discuss the problem with Ben. For she knew he would either criticize her for being too much of a worrier, or he would take the reins out of her hands and take care of whatever the problem was by himself. And she didn't want that. She knew she wasn't perfect at her job, but she didn't want Ben to take over for her. And, unfortunately, just as he had felt she wasn't "ready" for his love, she knew he often felt a need to mold her into what he wanted, into his image of her in a given situation. And she knew herself—and her abilities and needs and desires—better than he did.

And so, later that morning, when she called Ben to say the layouts were fine and the ads were ready to go, she said nothing about Kurt or his attempts to throw a wrench into the works.

CHAPTER EIGHT

Over the next few days Kate spoke with Ben often but didn't have time to see him. She was busy with advertising and public-relations work concerning the party at Xenon, and Ben was working nearly around the clock on a new car account.

But they talked daily, and their conversations were a delightful mix of business and pleasure, quick rundowns of the latest in the ad campaign along with quiet words of affection.

One afternoon, just as Kate was getting ready to leave Ivorsen and Shaw, Ben called and asked if she could stop by his apartment on her way to her dance class. Pleased, she agreed immediately; it had been a long time.

The moment he answered the door and she saw his face, she knew something was wrong. He looked haggard, worn, depressed. "Come on in," he said. From the look in his eyes she had thought he wasn't going to kiss her, had planned not to even touch her. But he caught her in his arms and kissed her long and hard, then looked into her eyes for a searching moment and drew her against his chest. "Oh, Kate," he said quietly, holding her tight against him.

"What is it?" she asked.

He looked down into her eyes and gently stroked her hair. "Come. We'll talk in here."

There was a fire going in the living room, and it looked warm and cozy, but Kate could think only that something was very, very wrong as she walked in with Ben and sat down next to him on the couch.

"Drink?" he asked.

She shook her head. "No, thanks. Tell me what's going on."

He stood and went over to the bar. "I think I'll have something after all," he said. He poured himself a glass of wine in silence and then came back to the couch. "I had a call at the office today," he said quietly, looking down into his glass and then into Kate's eyes. "From Celia." He took a sip of wine. "About Eliza, our daughter."

"What happened?" Kate asked.

He sighed. "Well. She's in high school, you know. Just a kid." He shook his head. "Sixteen years old. And it turns out she hasn't been going to school. Hasn't in weeks. Celia called me today about it, but it's been going on for weeks. Weeks!"

"Where has she been?" Kate asked.

"With friends. Kids she's gotten to be friends with this semester. And kids—obviously—who aren't going to be the best influence in the world on her." He took another sip of wine. "What infuriates me most about it is that Celia didn't even call me. I've been on the phone with both of them all evening, trying to come to some sort of . . . plan."

"When did Celia know about it?" Kate asked. "Maybe she just found out."

Ben shook his head. "Nope. She found out days ago.

She called me today because she went in to talk to the school principal, and he recommended that Eliza see someone professionally. *Then* she decided to call me." He stood up and walked over to the fireplace. "I just can't believe that my daughter is going through all that hell out there and I don't even know about it. I just don't understand what is in Celia's mind some of the time." He crouched down and threw another log on the flames, sending up a spray of sparks, and remained facing the fire.

Kate rose from the couch and walked over to him. "I'm sure Celia was upset," she said, kneeling down by his side. "As I would have been. And when you're upset, you do things that aren't necessarily rational. Or considerate. People do irrational things all the time."

"But dammit, Kate, I'm Eliza's father. It's just inconceivable to me how Celia could have 'forgotten.' Or even thought about it and decided she didn't want to let me know. I would never do a thing like that."

"You can't tell what you would do, really, until the time comes. Don't you think?"

He looked into her eyes. "Celia can make all the mistakes she wants as long as she doesn't make them with Eliza and Chris. That's all I ask."

"That's very easy for you to say," Kate said quietly, "since she's the one who's bringing them up, Ben. She *is* going to make mistakes."

He sighed and rubbed his face with his hands. When he turned, his eyes were red, and he looked more tired than she had ever seen him. "I'm going to go out there," he said. "For a few days, anyway, over Thanksgiving. How would you like to come with me?"

"I'd love to," she said.

His eyes studied hers. "Good," he said. "I'll take care of all the arrangements." He reached out and stroked her cheek. "I'll be glad to have you with me, Kate."

She smiled. "I'm glad. Now do you feel a little better, knowing that you're going?"

"I suppose," he said. "I'm very happy you'll be coming along, Kate. It'll give us some time together. But I won't really feel better until I talk to Eliza and spend some time with her." He sighed. "You know, sometimes I wonder if Celia and I shouldn't have stayed together just for the sake of the kids."

"I don't think that's usually too smart," Kate said. "In the end it hurts everyone. Anyway, Ben, from everything you've told me, your kids have turned out fine. Don't forget—Eliza is sixteen. No one's really happy or well-adjusted at sixteen. It's a really confusing age."

He smiled. "I wanted to run away and join the Foreign Legion when I was sixteen. I wasn't altogether sure what it was, but I wanted to live in the desert and meet beautiful women in smoky Moroccan tearooms and lead dangerous missions through casbahs and mountains and villages." He shook his head. "I spent the summer milking cows on my uncle's farm in North Carolina."

Kate laughed. "Well, that sounds kind of nice—to a city girl like me, anyway." She looked into his eyes, loving the way their amber warmth caressed her. "I'm glad you called, Ben," she said quietly. "We hadn't seen each other in so long I was beginning to think the phone was going to be our only means of communication." She smiled. "Not that it isn't nice talking to you, but—"

He smiled and gently stroked her cheek with a warm hand. "There *are* nicer things," he finished for her. "And

I wish you could stay," he said softly. "Celia's calling me back soon, but after that—"

She shook her head. "I have to go anyway," she said, covering his hand with hers. She loved its feel—man-rough yet tender—its scent, its touch. And as she gazed at this man she loved—his warm hazel eyes, his luxuriant dark hair, his rugged jawline—she was filled with happiness, and filled with wonder as well: for she hadn't let herself imagine that things would ever go this well. Soon she'd be going to California with him; and until then, they would be together as often as they could.

Kate left Ben's with a wonderful glow, a feeling that lasted during her dance class and on into the next day when she arrived at work. And the happiness she felt inside was matched by the energy at the store, as the night of the party at Xenon drew near. It was now only little more than a week away, and hundreds of people had been invited—including cosmetics and ready-to-wear clothing manufacturers, reporters from newspapers, women's magazines, radio, and TV, designers, jobbers, wholesalers, and models from two of the city's leading agencies. By the night of the party all of the invited guests would have received press kits filled with glossy copies of the forthcoming print ads, small soaps and colognes, and invitations to participate in the store's new personal shopping program which Ben had suggested and the board had just approved.

Kate had a wonderful feeling about the momentum that was building over the campaign, and she could feel it in the store as well, even though none of the ads had run yet. There was a different feeling in the air—an electricity, an excitement, created partly by the store's new look, partly by the new buying approach, and partly by the feeling that everyone was about to embark on a campaign that would bring lots and lots of new faces in to see what had been going on. Morale was far, far better, with salespeople taking a bit longer to show things to customers, and the new clothes that were in the store made an enormous difference in I and S's overall look. And over half the salespeople had signed up to be trained for the new personal shopping program.

A week before the party was to be held, shooting on the first series of sixty-second TV spots began.

Kate, Ben, Pierce, a free-lance makeup artist, and the Blake-Canfield director and stylist were all at a studio in the East Twenties—cold (the heating had broken), angry, and waiting what seemed like forever for Alexandra to get ready. The stylist had fixed Alexandra's clothes, the makeup artist had fixed her makeup, and the director had gone over her movements and lines dozens of times, but now all were waiting as Kurt talked to her in the back room of the loft. For the third time in ten minutes Alexandra had said she was ready, then burst into tears and gone running off to the back room. And for the third time Kurt was now in there with her, presumably trying to calm her down.

The director, Clyfford Grace, a young, reed-thin man who always had a cigarette or cup of coffee or both in his hands, jumped up from his chair and began pacing.

"What the hell is the matter with this kid?" he said, glaring at Ben and pacing away again. "I thought you said she was booked for a long-run campaign."

"She is," Ben said quietly, his voice full of irony.

"Christ, Austin, can't you do something? That art director *cum* rep *cum* God knows what can hardly be helping. *He* seems to be the reason she keeps falling apart."

Kate stood up. "I'll see what I can do," she said, and marched off toward the back room, uncertain of what approach would be best.

But as soon as she reached the partition and overheard what Kurt was saying, she knew what she would do.

"Come on, baby," he was cooing. But there was a razor's edge beneath the silk of his voice. "You know what will happen if this doesn't work out. Back to Kansas. No more city, no more me, no more glamor. You're right at the edge, baby. Screw it up and you're finished."

"But it's not fair," she sobbed. "I'm ex*hausted.* I told you that last night. Why can't I rest ever? If we hadn't stayed out till six, you know, maybe I wouldn't feel as if I'm completely falling apart."

Kate had heard enough. She knocked on the partition and looked in.

Kurt and Alexandra were sitting on the bed, Kurt closest to the door, his body positioned as if to shield Alexandra from danger. When Kate stepped in, Kurt looked at her with cool annoyance.

"Kurt, please leave us alone for a few minutes," Kate said firmly.

He jerked his head back in surprise. But before he could say anything more, she put a hand on his shoulder. "Now," she said. "It's time for some girl talk."

He pressed his lips together, and she could see him weighing his options. He had always, she realized now, been transparent in this way, showing what he was thinking at any given moment. "All right," he said, standing up. "Just make sure you don't say anything to upset her."

Kate gave him a withering look and then turned to Alexandra as Kurt left and closed the door. "What's bothering you?" she asked gently. "Aside from the pressures of the shooting, I mean."

Alexandra looked up with eyes brimming with tears. "It *is* the shooting. Kurt said if I ruin this, there won't be anything ever again."

Kate sighed. "Look. It *is* important that you do well, Alexandra. But you don't have to do well on the first take. See what it's like working with the director instead of trying to work with Kurt. Believe me, Clyfford Grace has had a lot more experience than Kurt Reeves. And see what it's like trying to please yourself instead of Kurt. Think about what *you* want and how you want to act."

Alexandra frowned. "But I want to do well for *him,*" she said. "You used to go out with him, didn't you—?"

Kate nodded, wondering what else Kurt had told her.

"How can you work with him?" Alexandra asked. "I mean, if he broke up with *me,* I don't know what I'd do."

Kate hesitated, deciding to let it pass. "You do what you have to, Alexandra. And when you know what you want out of your work and your life, it makes things a lot easier. So do me a favor and try—just try—not to think about Kurt when you go out there. Just do what you think is best."

Alexandra nodded and smiled. "Okay. I promise I'll try. But could I talk to Kurt for just a sec before I go out there again?"

"Oh—" She sighed. "Make it fast. I'll get him for you."

Kate went out and sent Kurt back in, then walked over to where Ben and Clyff were drinking coffee by the floor-to-ceiling windows at the far end of the loft. "Well, she should be out in a minute," Kate said. "Kurt has obviously put her under too much pressure. This *is* her first assignment, you know. But I think she'll be fine."

Ben slammed down his cup. "Dammit, Kate, I think you were right at the beginning. Alexandra Dayton just might not be worth the trouble she's going to cause."

"I was worried about Dick Dayton back then," she said. "And he's hardly said a word. *I* think she'll be fine. If we give her a chance and try to minimize Kurt's influence."

"Kurt," Ben growled, turning away. He stalked over to the far window and stood with his back to Kate and Clyff.

Kate walked over to Ben. "What's the matter with you?" she asked. "You're acting as if this is a major crisis."

He turned and looked at her with blazing eyes. "Maybe it is," he seethed. "You wouldn't know it. The girl is a flake, and you're such a softhearted . . . sentimentalist that you refuse to see the handwriting on the wall even when the letters are ten feet high."

She stared at him. "And what is it that you know?" she demanded. "I'm the one who was in there talking to her."

He sighed. "All right. Maybe she's okay. For now. But we *can*not have delays like this again. It's one thing—a very expensive one for you—to keep a director waiting. But in terms of public relations, Kate, it will be worse in two weeks, when you've got a crowd of people in your 'Nighttime Secrets' sleepwear department waiting to meet Alexandra and Pierce, and no one's there but Pierce and a nervous assistant buyer explaining to the crowd that they've missed their lunch hours but the show *won't* go on."

"Ben, this is *one* time. Her first shooting."

"And that will be her first in-store promotion," he said. "And the same thing could happen."

"That is *not* your area," she said. "The promotions were part of your overall plan, but they're run by my department and you don't even know half of—"

"Kate," he interrupted, looking at her curiously. "Don't you see? I'm trying to help you. I don't want some masochistic little fool throwing a wrench in your success. I want everything to go smoothly."

"And it will," she said. "And really, Ben. You could try to be nicer about it. If she had overheard what you just said, she'd have been crushed. What's wrong with you?"

He shook his head, sighing. "Sorry. I guess—well, for one thing, whether you accept it or not, I *am* tense because it's your project. I want it perfect, Kate. Perfect. And also, I happen to have stopped smoking this morning." He smiled. "After fifteen years."

"Really? That's great! But why? I mean why today?"

"I've been trying every day since the other night, when I was trying to talk to you and I couldn't even concentrate because you had asked me not to smoke—or to wait. I could hardly speak after that—and I decided it was a habit that had much too much power over me. Anyway, I tried to quit for a few days, but I kept finding conveniently hidden pouches of tobacco all over the apartment. But this morning I decided today was the day. And I think it is."

"That's wonderful," she said.

"Only if I don't keep snapping at you," he answered, smiling.

"Don't worry," she said. "I'll hit you if you do it again."

He looked past her then, and she turned and saw Alexandra and Kurt coming out of the back room. Alexandra looked much more relaxed—almost calm—and Kate looked up at Ben. "See? She'll be fine."

And, despite all the pre-session tears and tensions, the shooting went well. Alexandra listened to Clyfford Grace carefully, almost as if trying to understand a foreign language, and Kurt stayed in the background most of the time, "correcting" only one or two changes the stylist had made while he was talking to Alexandra.

Alexandra was good—better when she didn't listen to Kurt, best when the cameras began rolling. And Pierce was his usual excellent self, getting better and better each time.

By the end of the afternoon, they had a series of thirty- and sixty-second spots that would be shown both on television and in short segments at the party on Tuesday night. Kate felt it had been an excellent session, and judging by everyone's expression—everyone except Kurt, of course—the feeling was unanimous.

Kate and Ben left the studio together and, once out on the street, began walking arm in arm.

"What's on with you for the rest of the afternoon?" he asked as they headed toward Second Avenue.

"Oh, about a thousand phone calls. I'm following up on the invitations to the party Tuesday night—making sure people got all the invitations and all that."

"You?" he asked. "What about your assistant? And your secretary, for that matter?"

"They're doing some," she said. "But I want to do a lot of it myself. A little personal contact never hurt, you know. A lot of people respond to that sort of thing."

"Mm, I know," he said, pulling her close and sending a thrill of desire through her. He stopped and turned, looking into her eyes. "When am I going to see you, Kate? I feel as if we've created a monster: we're both so busy because of the damn campaign that we never see each other outside of studios and offices."

She smiled. "I know. It's ridiculous."

"But what about us? I've got to fly out to Michigan this evening to meet with a client. I'll be back Monday, but—"

"Why not this afternoon?" she said. "I feel the same way, you know. I just want to . . . hold you in my arms. It's been so long."

"Well. Monday," he said quietly.

She blinked. "Fine. But what about this afternoon?"

He shook his head. "I'd love to. But I can wait, Kate, and so can you."

She stared at him. "Are you serious? You mean because of my work? Isn't that for me to determine?"

He looked into her eyes. "I want you to understand something," he said. "I guess I really haven't made it clear." He glanced at the passing crowds, then back at Kate. "I love you, Kate. I've been waiting for someone like you to come along—looking for someone like you for years. I love all kinds of things about you—your moods, your looks, your strengths, and one of the things that first caught my eye was something I thought of as a paradox—this beautiful young woman who's so strong in business and so vulnerable and giving underneath. But, Kate, sometimes the line between those two fades. You're too ready to give in, too ready to empathize with someone like Alexandra Dayton."

"I don't really see what that has to do with us," she said. "Not that I even agree with what you're saying, by the way."

He sighed. "It's a perfect example," he said. "I want to see you, you want to see me, and you're willing to jeopardize your job instead of waiting."

Her eyes widened. "If you could hear yourself," she said quietly. "You know what, Ben? I just realized something about you: you are a complete and total perfectionist. I can't think of one instance as I look back when you haven't expected everyone and everything around you to be perfect. And look—this morning you chipped another imperfection off your perfect self—you stopped smoking. You don't need a lover, Ben; you need some sort of plaything you can work on to your heart's content—someone who doesn't mind changing just to please you. But that isn't me."

"Kate—"

"I mean it," she said.

"But it's such a minor thing."

"Then, why couldn't you let it go?" she demanded. "You can't have it both ways, Ben. If my staying or going to work for the next couple of hours is such a minor thing, then why couldn't you have let it go and said nothing?"

"Because I have to be honest with you."

"Oh, come on," she said. " 'Being honest' is usually just an excuse to say something the other person doesn't want to hear."

Ben frowned. "Kate, I— Is that how you really feel? That I want to say something you don't want to hear?"

"All I know is that you can't seem to accept me as I am from one day to the next. In bed we're just great together—but I can't keep this up if I feel you're trying to . . . remold me every time you see me at work or in action."

She searched his eyes, fighting the memory of lovemaking. "I can't see you if it's going to be on that level."

"Don't say that," he said, taking her by the shoulders.

She resisted the warmth of his touch, resisted the honeyed pull of his eyes. "What do you suggest?" she asked hollowly. "I'm telling you how I feel, Ben. You have to say more than 'don't say that.' "

"All right—let's grab a taxi and we'll go to my place."

Her eyes widened. "Oh, forget it," she breathed. "God! Do you really think we're still talking about this afternoon, Ben?"

"I don't know," he said loudly. "Kate, I don't know how to please you. You want to get together, and I say I think you should work. But when I agree, you don't want to see me anymore."

She shook her head. "Uh-uh. Not so. *I'm* the one who doesn't know how to please you. You know, the first time we talked, you said you didn't mean to sound sanctimonious, but that you had never looked at another woman when you were first married. At the time I had found that difficult to believe. Everyone's human, after all—if only in terms of fantasizing. But you probably *didn't* look at anyone else, out of sheer determination." She could see the pain in his eyes, but she went on. It was the only way she would get through to him, the only way she would break through the problem. "You're so controlled; every part of your life is so planned and programed that you probably are as perfect as you want to be. And now you want some perfect woman to fit into your life. But dammit, Ben, I don't want to be with you if I'm always feeling that you're trying to change me."

His eyes were dark and unreadable. "Well," he said

quietly. "It seems you haven't been as happy as I thought. Or as happy as I've been." He looked past her, and then into her eyes. "What do you suggest?"

They were alarming words, and she could say nothing at first. "I—I don't know."

He searched her eyes. "I hadn't realized you were unhappy."

"I'm not," she said, and then shook her head. "Or I am. But not . . ." Her voice trailed off. "I don't know what to say."

His gaze was sad, serious. "I've told you before," he said quietly. "I don't believe in forcing issues or people or things. If you're unhappy, Kate, then this relationship isn't worth a damn." His gaze was deep and powerful, as deep and powerful as their lovemaking had been. She wanted to tell him to forget what she had said, but she couldn't; for she knew she had been right. "I think we both have some thinking to do," he said, brushing a wisp of her bangs back. "I'll be in Michigan for the next few days, but I'll be back on Monday. I hope I can see you then. And I hope you still plan on coming with me to California." And he turned and walked away, up Second Avenue into the autumn wind.

Kate wanted to call out to him, to stop him. But what could she say? He was right: she *was* unhappy. She was the one who had brought it up. And she did have some thinking to do. But as she watched him walk away, head down and shoulders hunched against the cold, she felt as if a part of her heart had just been cut out.

Kate walked back to Ivorsen and Shaw, though it was cold and rather a long distance. But she needed time to think, to snap out of the haze that had fallen over her as she had watched Ben walk away. The haze was part panic, part fear, a terrible feeling of emptiness that had closed over her soul like a chill gray mist.

For she had no idea how Ben had felt as he walked off into the cold. He had said he hoped she still planned on coming to California; but did he really? He wouldn't have even brought it up unless at some level he hoped she wouldn't come. God—what had she done?

But she shed no tears. For there was a part of her that knew she had done the right thing. She had just taken a painful step she had never taken before. With Kurt and other boyfriends, she had never stood up for herself. Each in his own way had tended to be very dominating, and, translating this into caring, Kate had accepted it. She had told herself that Kurt or Alan or Steve or whoever wouldn't care about what she wore or said or did if he didn't love her. And over and over again, she had failed to see it wasn't true caring.

She remembered how Kurt would lie on her bed as she got dressed before a night out on the town, and she would have to try on six different outfits before he finally said one looked good. Something about this had made her feel loved; she felt he was doing it because he was proud of her, and he wanted her to look her best. But now, as she looked back on it all, she saw how wrong she had been. Yes, Kurt had wanted her to look good, but only so that *he* could look good. And he had rarely complimented her, either—perhaps out of the fear that if she became too confident, she would leave him. And this had happened—in different ways—over and over again with all the men Kate had ever been involved with.

And now she had stood up for herself.

She knew that Ben's criticisms weren't of the self-serving nature that Kurt's had been. But even so, they hurt, and they rankled. Why did she have to be perfect? And what was so wrong with what she did? This was a new period of her life—a period of strength, of standing up for herself. And Ben would have to see that.

When Kate got back to the store, she went straight to Alison's office, in credit operations on the eighth floor.

Kate sat down at her friend's desk and listened to the tag end of Alison's conversation with a customer who had defaulted on a payment.

Kate smiled and shook her head as Alison hung up the phone. "I don't know how you do it."

"Well, I'll tell you a secret. When I want to be nasty, it helps if I pretend they're my last rotten boyfriend. Or my first husband's new wife. Or I could take *all* of your exes, Kate." She smiled and exhaled a long stream of smoke. "Speaking of whom. Or which, I should say in this case. I heard some interesting news."

"What?"

"Well. Again, this is third- or fourth-hand, but your little ex-charmer Kurt Reeves is in the hot seat right now. *Really* touch and go, Kate."

Kate smiled. "Great. Why?"

"Well, it seems that he's made no secret of the fun he's having with Miss Tiny Tears—what's her name?—Alexandra Dayton. And not only fun—but he seems to have become her rep."

"I know."

Alison smiled. "Needless to say, this news doesn't sit

too well with our favorite v.p.-operations, Mr. Richard Dayton. According to my sources he's livid. Kurt's chances of getting the art directorship are less than zero right now, and as soon as they can hire someone else, he's out."

"Really?"

"*Plus*—and you'll get a kick out of this, I think—Dayton 'ordered' Alexandra to stop seeing Kurt and she refused."

Kate shook her head. "Poor kid. She's really still a kid, you know. She's completely taken with Kurt. Everything she does on the set has to be 'okay with Kurt.' She's totally passive. And I really don't envy the position she's in right now—being pulled by Kurt in one direction and by her marvelous uncle in the other."

Alison nodded. "I know. But look—better her than you, right?"

"Definitely. Except that I seem to have a problem of my own."

Alison raised a brow. "Ben?"

Kate nodded.

"Mr. Perfect? Ben Austin? What's the matter?"

"You just said it," Kate said. "Mr. Perfect. It's the most ridiculous of ironies. All my life I've been attracted to guys who are wrong for me in some way. Finally, through some miracle, I find one who seems great: he likes me; he's not afraid of commitment; he's wonderful in every way. Nothing wrong with him, right?" She shook her head. "He's very sure of himself, Ally. And he's very sure that he wants someone in his life. But he's so damn sure of those things that what he's looking for just doesn't exist. He wants the perfect woman. Someone strong, apparently, but I think he wants someone he can control as well. And he expects me to be it." She gave an ironic smile. "And as you and I know all too well, Ally, I ain't perfect."

Alison sighed and put out her cigarette. "Men. What pains."

"I know!" Kate said. "And if this had happened six months ago, I would have gone along with it: 'Yes, Ben, no, Ben, oh, you're right, Ben.' Except that that doesn't work. If you're molding your personality according to what you think your man wants, then you're not even really *with* him. He's having a relationship with someone who's playing a role. And then the whole thing falls apart." She sighed. "And I don't want that to happen with Ben."

"Have you told him all this?"

Kate shrugged. "Some. But it's hard to say, when you're feeling it most strongly. Anyway, he's going to be away for a few days. And that'll give us both time to do some thinking."

"Well, it sounds tough, Kate, but don't let him give you any crap. You had enough with Kurt to last a lifetime. And if Ben can't deal with your standing up for yourself, to hell with him."

"Right," Kate said absently, wishing it were all as easy as it sounded.

When she went back to her office and immersed herself in the task of calling selected names on her guest list, her spirits lifted. Naturally, representatives of the major newspapers would be at the party—not because Ivorsen and Shaw was a big advertiser, but because the event and its invitees would make interesting coverage in either the gossip column or, in the case of the *Times,* "The Evening Hours." Kate hoped that eventually the store's resurgence would be covered in the business pages, too, but felt it would be just as well if that coverage came a bit later, when there was good rather than bad news to report.

All the women's magazines were sending people from their fashion and beauty departments, though the event would be more one of goodwill than coverage. As national magazines they would be unlikely actually to write anything about this store which existed only in New York City. But their presence meant something special to the manufacturers and designers who would be there. Staff members from most of the cosmetics companies whose products the store carried were coming, too, and some of them—those whose counters were manned by their own employees rather than employees of Ivorsen and Shaw—were already intimately involved with the revamping of the store.

By the end of the afternoon Kate had called most of the people she had wanted to call, with good results. They were all naturally excited about the new campaign: more customers at Ivorsen and Shaw meant more buyers, ultimately, for their products. The momentum was definitely building.

And a few days before the party the ads came out. Store attendance was up, morale was up, and Kate received enthusiastic compliments on the ads from every board member including Dayton.

The day before the party Blake-Canfield sent over a tape presentation they had prepared for it. The presentation was a series of quick shots of Alexandra and Pierce spliced in with shots of the store's different departments and boutiques, and it was going to be shown continuously on the far wall of the discotheque. Kate was surprised at how good it looked even without the accompanying music; the audio-visual people at the agency had done a beautiful job, and she felt better than ever about the following evening.

The only part that she dreaded was facing Ben. Now that she had spoken up, what came next? Would Ben change? Would he want to change? Had the sadness in his eyes come from a realization that the relationship could never go anywhere?

Kate wasn't certain she wanted to know the answers. Because she knew that, no matter what problems there were, and no matter what conflicts existed, she loved him. And part of her wished she had never said anything at all.

CHAPTER NINE

Kate thought she would hear from Ben when he returned from Michigan Monday afternoon; he wasn't the type to leave anything unresolved, and she knew he would want to talk before the party Tuesday night. But he didn't call.

And his words kept coming back to her: "This relationship isn't worth a damn." But it wasn't true! She had been trying to be constructive, to face something that was bothering her. But in Ben's quest for perfection, perhaps he felt it was time to move on.

When Kate walked into her building and greeted the doorman, she remembered the night Ben had come without calling. Would that happen tonight? Or perhaps he had called and left a message on her answering machine. Well, if he hadn't, she would call him. If he was back in the city, there was no reason not to try to talk things through.

Kate's answering machine indicated there was one message, and Kate set the tape for "play" and sat on the edge of the couch next to the machine to listen.

But it wasn't Ben. "Kate? This is Mother. I know it's been a long time, but . . . it's two weeks till Thanksgiving, and I wanted to know whether you were coming.

. . . I hope everything is okay. Please call when you can. I love you."

Kate turned off the machine and sank back into the couch. Damn. Now she didn't know what to tell her mother; it all depended on what Ben had to say.

Kate had never been overjoyed by the holiday season anyway, even as a child. She had seen Thanksgiving and Christmas as days on which she was expected to be happy, days on which she had to pretend and force a smile. That had changed somewhat when she had left home, and since Kate had begun working at Ivorsen and Shaw, the holidays had meant good things in terms of work: business increased tremendously, the ad budget skyrocketed for a month, and there was a genuinely happy if somewhat frenetic atmosphere at the store.

But there had been the visits to her mother as well: strained visits in which there had been little to say, less to be happy about. Now, perhaps it would be a little easier with her mother's new husband. Nevertheless, it was not something Kate looked forward to.

She dialed Ben's number instead. Even that was easier than facing the prospect of what was sure to be a difficult call.

"Hello?" Oh, that voice she loved.

"Hi, it's Kate."

"Hey, I'm glad you called," he said. He sounded as if he were smiling, and her spirits leaped.

"I thought you might like to come over," she said.

"I'd love to. Have you eaten?"

"Nope."

"Chinese okay?"

"Sounds great," she said, and hung up a few moments later.

The moment Kate saw Ben when she opened the door, her only conscious thought was that she loved him.

But she followed his lead. He kissed her lightly, put the bags of containered food on the foyer table, and gave her his coat almost formally.

And then, in the living room on the couch, when he said, "I've been doing a lot of thinking," she felt as if her stomach had dropped out.

God, she thought. *It's over.*

"I'll make us some drinks," she said, and stood.

"No. Wait," he said. "Now, Mr. Perfect here did without a smoke when you wanted to talk. We can talk without a drink." He held up his hand to prevent her interrupting him. "And don't go accusing me of trying to be perfect again, Kate. I just want to talk now because you look about the way I felt these past few days, and I want to get this all out into the open. Now, sit. Please."

She sank onto the couch.

"Thank you. That was perfect." He smiled. "Now I'll say what I have to say, and then—I don't know. All we can do is see what's what. I did a lot of thinking out in Michigan. And a lot of missing you, Kate. I missed what I love about you, I even missed the things I had criticized you for. That's all I know, darling. I missed you like hell. I can't deny what you said the other day—I *am* looking for someone perfect. Perfect for *me.* And I don't see anything wrong with that. I love you, Kate. If it bothers you that much when I criticize you over something you're doing at your job, or when I think you're doing yourself a disservice in some way, I promise I'll try not to do that.

But I can't hold back and keep my feelings to myself. On the job, I'll leave it to you, but I'm never going to stop telling you how I feel. That's all—and the best—I can do. And I do want you to come with me over the holidays, Kate."

She smiled. "I—that sounds better," she said, relaxing into the cushions of the couch. She realized her whole body had been tensed since he had come in, and only now was she beginning to unwind. "I'm sorry I said I thought you thought you were perfect. I didn't really mean it."

"Did you miss me?" he asked, looking at her in challenge.

"Of course," she said. And she smiled. "Even at work."

He shot her a look of mock warning. "Don't tell me about work unless you want to hear what I have to say," he said. "Remember, I never promised to be mute."

She laughed. "I know. But I did want to tell you that the ads look beautiful," she said, smiling into his eyes. "And the tape presentation was amazing. I can't wait for the party."

"I'm glad," he said. "I looked the tapes over today and I thought they looked pretty good. Alexandra and Pierce are both stunners."

"Let's hope they stay that way. Or that Alexandra does. Pierce I'm not too worried about."

"You're worried about Alexandra's involvement with Kurt?"

Kate nodded. "She's very vulnerable, Ben. She projects such self-assurance and confidence in front of a camera that it's easy to forget she's very young for her age. Obviously very sheltered, too. And Kurt is throwing her onto the fast track of New York nightlife just a little too quickly."

Ben shook his head. "What a waste," he said. He sighed and looked into her eyes. "You know, there's something I don't understand, Kate. Every time I've been around Kurt, I've tried to see what you saw in him. Aside from his looks, of course."

She smiled. "Can't a woman go out with a man for his looks?" she asked teasingly.

"Of course. But I don't think that was true of you," he said, apparently unwilling to let her joke the question away.

"Well," she said, "it's not that easy for me to say, really. But initially it *was* Kurt's looks that attracted me. We didn't meet at the store, actually. We met at a party given by a woman who works at I and S. Anyway, he was very attractive to me. I wasn't looking for anything really serious. But we were . . ." Her voice trailed off as she looked into Ben's eyes. It was difficult to talk about Kurt with him, to look at feelings she hadn't wanted to look at in a while. "Let's just say there was an attraction. And he seemed like a challenge at the time. He was new at the store, and very cocky, very seductive with all the women at this party. I felt the glove had been thrown down in challenge, and I wanted to be the one to pick it up." She smiled. "Or pick *him* up. At the time I thought it was quite an achievement. There were a lot of broken hearts that night, and mine wasn't one of them."

"That doesn't sound like you," Ben said.

"Well, it was true," she said. "Even if you don't like the sound of it," she added quietly. "What's ironic, though, is that with other men I've gone out with, when we broke up, that was that. I didn't see them again. But with Kurt still at the store, and with another woman, it's given me a chance I've never had before. I look at the way he acts with Alexandra—very dominating, almost cruel—and I can see that he did the same with me." She smiled. "Which is all consistent with my unbeatable taste in men."

"And what about me?" Ben asked softly. "You talk about how you were attracted to Kurt almost as a challenge. He was someone you had to get just to see if you could. And it doesn't sound as if you liked him much. But what about me?"

She smiled into his eyes. "You were different," she said softly.

"I'm glad," he said. And his eyes shone with desire, communicating deeply and persuasively that he wanted her. "Kate," he said softly. "Come."

He led her off to the bedroom, and they undressed by the light of the moon. He lay back on the bed and she came up after him, coming into his arms and resting her cheek on his chest. "Yes, you were different," she said, running a hand along his chest. "I liked you. But you were a challenge, too."

She sat up then, wanting to look into his eyes. "And at some level, somehow, I knew how good all this would be."

He smiled. "Making love?"

"Yes." She smiled and swung a leg over him so she was astride him, her softness against the hardness of his frame. "When did you know?" she asked, looking into his eyes.

He reached out, playing with the soft orbs of her breasts, flicking at her nipples with his fingers.

"When do you think?" he asked.

She shrugged. "I don't know."

He smiled. "The moment I saw you," he said, and then he inhaled deeply, his eyes roving across her breasts. "I felt so sure," he said, putting his warm hands on her thighs. She moved forward, wanting to be closer, and he coaxed his hands up along her inner thighs. "I was so sure," he said huskily, "but even so, I had no idea that you'd be so . . . so beautiful . . . so giving . . . so responsive." His warm, strong fingers began to weave their spell, and she was filled with a simmering ache for him, awash with overwhelming desire. She rolled her head back in pleasure. "Oh, Ben," she whispered.

She let her hands trail back, over the hard strength of his thighs, questing for his firm desire. She was caught up in a smoldering burning, searing with desire for the fulfilment she knew he could give her. And he guided her back, his hands over the softness of her hips as he lifted her and, with a surge, entered in a burst of pleasure. "Yes, yes," she groaned, as with his hands he set the rhythm of their passion, as she let the flame burning within consume her. His hands moved up then, over her breasts, over her nipples, and for a moment she looked down into his eyes with wondrous joy. And then deep, deep pleasure took over as Kate and Ben cried out for each other, quickened their thrusting union in melting, dissolving heat that turned to pulsating, shuddering ecstasy.

After whispered words of love, they both fell into deep, comfortable sleeps, their bodies draped around each other in complete satisfaction, total relaxation. When Kate awakened, the room was dark, the light of the moon slanting in and lighting Ben's handsome face.

Kate rolled over and looked at the clock. Five after eleven. And then she remembered she hadn't called her mother. It was too late to call tonight, of course. Which meant she'd have to call tomorrow from work, when the office would be particularly hectic.

Ben shifted and pulled her close so she fit perfectly against his body, her back snug against the warmth of his chest. "There must be some very cold Chinese food somewhere in this house," he said.

"I'm starved. Stay right where you are and I'll bring it in."

"Cold?" he asked.

"Sure, it's great. Trust me."

"I do," he said. "I mean, I know. I just didn't know anyone agreed with me." He kissed the back of her neck. "But then, if anyone did, it would be you," he said, and kissed her again.

A few minutes later they were sitting up in bed with two ice-cold Kirin beers and cold but delicious moo shu pork, hunan beef with bamboo shoots and watercress, stir-fried spicy chicken and sautéed snow peas and water chestnuts.

"Mm. Fantastic," Ben said between mouthfuls. "So what else happened while I was gone and missing you?"

"Oh—" She hesitated. "Well, my mother called, wanting to know if I was coming to Connecticut for Thanksgiving."

"And—?"

"Well, I didn't exactly call her back yet."

"Why not?"

"Well, I didn't know what I was going to do—whether we were going to go to California together or not."

"Are you going to call her tomorrow?"

"Sure. From work."

He sighed. "If I hadn't asked you to come with me, would you have gone to see her?"

She shrugged. "I guess."

He looked at her skeptically. "You 'guess'? Does that mean yes or no, Kate?"

She let the forkful of chicken she had been about to eat hang in midair. "You're asking an awful lot of questions," she said. "I hardly need to have my mother call, with you around."

His eyes flashed. "All right, fine," he said. "We won't talk about work and we won't talk about your mother. Is that what you want?"

She sighed. "No. And I'm sorry. I just dread visiting, that's all. This new man she's married—I just know it's not going to work out, and I hate being witness to it, seeing her trying to be happy over something that's doomed." She looked into Ben's eyes. "But let's talk about it some other time, okay? I'm just really glad you're here and I don't want to—" She shrugged, hoping he wouldn't press her further.

He studied her eyes, amber searching brown in a deep gaze that made her strangely self-conscious all of a sudden. "When did your mother move up to Connecticut?" he asked.

"Oh, a few years ago," Kate said, pouring the rest of her beer into her glass. She had wanted to talk about something else; but for now, the subject seemed neutral enough, and she went on: "When her company moved out of the city, she moved with it. And I guess it was a good move in terms of where she's living. I just—I just don't happen to visit her much."

He reached out and gently touched her cheek. "Do you think you can try to go out and see her before we leave?"

"I don't know," Kate said, not altogether truthfully.

He sighed. "I know you and your mother don't get along, Kate. But I can't help thinking if you spent more time . . ." His voice trailed off. "You know, with both my parents dead, it's very difficult for me to see you and your mother blithely going along without making any kind of effort to—"

"Blithely?" she interrupted. "How do you know I'm blithely going along? Don't you think it bothers me that I basically have no family, that the one person around—my mother—is someone I don't get along with?"

"Then, why don't you try?"

"I *have* tried," she said. "And someday I'll try again. But we don't get along, all right? Sometimes you have to accept things like that, Ben, whether you want to or not. Life is not perfect. Families do break apart, kids do go wrong, things that aren't very nice happen all the time. And I resent your assuming that you're the only one bothered by these things. I wish I did have a real family, and I wish I did get along with my mother. But I'm not going to spend all my time thinking about it, Ben."

He searched her eyes. "But what exactly is it?" he asked. "*How* is it that you don't get along?"

"That really would take all night to explain," she said, looking away.

"I'm not going anywhere," he said softly.

She turned and met his gaze. She had the unwelcome sense that he was probing, that she would open herself up to him and that at the most unexpected of moments, after calm words of encouragement and empathy, he would suddenly come out with a criticism. "I think some other time would be better," she said.

"All right. I just thought it might help. Because"—he hesitated—"you know, we do tend to repeat family patterns. You marry people formed from the images of your own parents and other people you've known, and much of the time you just repeat your own parents' experience. And it seems to me that—"

"That you're about to say something I've thought of myself and would rather not dwell on," she interrupted. "Yes, I don't have much to work with in terms of a family model. Since my father left us and my mother proceeded to go out with and marry another series of equally winning types, the chances of my following that pattern and being happy aren't too great. But plenty of people have done it, Ben. Women whose parents have had terrible marriages and messy divorces have had wonderful relationships and marriages of their own, and the same is true with men. So it doesn't necessarily follow, and it doesn't necessarily help me to think about it that much. I don't have to repeat my mother's experience, you know."

"But don't you see that you are?" he asked softly.

"What?"

"Don't you see that you're doing just that, Kate? Doing just what your mother does—choosing men who are sure to run off, who are sure not to work out."

She stared at him. "I see you have it all figured out for me," she said quietly. "I hadn't known I was such a predetermined and easy-to-understand case history."

"I never said that," he replied.

"Well, then, tell me something," she said quietly. "If

you really think that I'm doing what you say—what does that make you, Ben?"

"We're not talking about me," he said.

"*I* am. You're so sure I've got rotten judgment, Ben. Then, what does that make you? Are you one of the men who run off or one of the men who don't?"

"That depends on both of us, Kate. Not just me. That's what I'm talking about. I don't think you trust anybody enough to make any kind of commitment. Not yet. And you won't until you face the fact that you've got a rough history to get over."

"Thanks a lot," she said. "God, Ben, I had no idea you thought you were going out with—"

"Stop it," he interrupted. "You're misunderstanding me. I only want to bring this up because it's important to me; *you're* important to me. I love you, Kate." His eyes met hers, and for a moment their gaze melted into deep heat. "I love you," he said more softly. "But making love is the only time I feel you're really mine. The rest of the time it's as if you're fighting me out of deep, deep mistrust."

"I don't know why that surprises you," she said, her voice hoarse with sudden anger. "Occasionally—usually during an argument—you tell me you love me. Yet most of the time, you're tearing me down. It doesn't matter if it's what I do at work, or my feelings about men, or even my past; I can't seem to do anything right for you, Ben." She ignored the look of pained surprise in his eyes and went on. "You've always struck me as very steady, very secure, someone with his feet very much on the ground, and you presented yourself that way as well: someone, you said, who was looking for a woman to share his life with.

But I wonder whether that's even true. You're the one who's driving me away. And I don't think I want to go to California with you, either. I wanted to go with a man I loved and who loved me—not an analyst who's going to pick apart everything I say and do and feel." She put her glass down on the night table and turned to face Ben more directly. "I don't know how I feel about you right now, Ben. All I know is that I don't think we should see each other for a while. It would be too easy—much too easy—to make everything all right by making love and capturing whatever seems to be eluding us outside of bed; but that wouldn't be fair to either of us." She couldn't bear to look at him anymore; his face seemed to be crumbling beneath her words, dissolving into pain she didn't want to see.

"Kate," he pleaded, reaching for her hand.

She turned away and got off the bed. She grabbed a robe from her closet door and hastily put it on, then turned and faced Ben. "I mean it," she said, her gaze steady.

"When, then?" he asked. "What are you saying? How long do you need, Kate?"

"I don't know," she said quietly as she turned away.

She heard him get off the bed, heard him walk around gathering his clothes. She walked out at that point, feeling a stranger in her own apartment, standing outside the bedroom as if she didn't belong. For suddenly everything seemed different, frightening, unpredictable. Ben was in there getting dressed, and she had no idea what had just happened—except that he was leaving, that he wasn't coming back.

As she turned to face the bedroom, Ben came striding

toward her. She looked up at him for one hopeful moment, but his eyes were cold and hard.

And he walked past her, as if she hadn't even been standing there. And as she heard the door shut softly behind her, her heart went cold with panic.

He had left without a word, without a softening glance, without a moment's hesitation. He was gone.

Kate hardly slept that night, tormented by what had happened and what she had to face. For nothing lay ahead except deep uncertainty. Tomorrow night she would see Ben at the party. And with sickening dread she knew the experience wouldn't be anything but painful.

The next morning, when Kate arrived at Ivorsen and Shaw a bit before the doors opened to the public, the store was alive with anticipation over the night's party. Saleswomen who lived in other boroughs of the city had brought the dresses they were going to wear that night, and in the elevators, offices, and ladies' rooms, all talk was of the party.

Kate moved through as if in a dream, weighed down by turmoil and confusion. The joy and anticipation in the air meant nothing to her now; all she felt in relation to the party was dread.

Yet she managed to hold her emotions in check enough to get what she had to do over with. In the early afternoon she sent Linda down to Xenon by taxi to make sure that the VIP tables were being properly set off with "reserved" cards and that all the preparations were going smoothly. Though the party was a joint project handled by Kate's department, Blake-Canfield, and Ivorsen and Shaw's home entertaining consultant, Kate had the ultimate responsibility for the party's success or failure, and she felt it would be an important act of strength to keep things running smoothly despite the state she was in.

And then, when Kate realized she had managed to "forget" to call her mother three times already that day, she finally called. The conversation was strained and brief, but Kate managed to stay outwardly calm and unemotional for most of it. The only point when the tension broke out into the open was when her mother—now Mrs. Creasey—asked whether Kate would be coming alone.

"Yes," Kate said evenly.

"Oh." There was a long pause. Then: "No boyfriend?"

"I—yes, I'm involved with someone, Mother," Kate said, wishing she knew whether that were even true anymore.

"Why don't you bring him, then?"

"Well, I don't think so."

"Oh. So he's just casual, then."

"No, not really," Kate said, her voice slightly raised. "I just don't think I'll bring him."

"It isn't a long drive, Kate. Just an hour and a half."

"I know," Kate said. "That has nothing to do with it, Mother. I'm coming alone. And if I change my mind, I'll let you know, okay?"

"I'd love to meet him, Kate. It's been so long since I've met any of your boyfriends."

"I know," Kate said. "I know." And after another five minutes, she managed—finally—to say good-bye.

Kate hung up and sighed. Everything had changed so quickly, so drastically. The holiday she had looked forward to would now be completely different from what she had planned, and tonight—a night that was supposed to be a celebration, a night of triumph—was sure to be an evening marked by anger and sadness, awkwardness and uncertainty.

But she managed. Late in the afternoon she met with Pierce and Alexandra to go over their duties for the evening. Alexandra looked exhausted, with dark circles under her eyes that even makeup couldn't hide; and she didn't seem to be getting along with Pierce as well as usual. After Kate had said all she wanted to, she sent Pierce away and spoke with Alexandra alone.

"What's wrong?" Kate asked. "You look terrible."

Alexandra looked crushed, and Kate hurried to soften her words. "Not *ter*rible, Alexandra, but terrible for you." She paused. "Maybe I can help if you tell me what's wrong."

Alexandra quickly shook her head. "It's just part of the business," she said mechanically, as if repeating words she had heard many times before. "I'll take a nap this afternoon and I promise I'll look fine." She stood up. "So actually, I'd better go now."

"Okay," Kate said. "I'll see you at Xenon, then. The car will pick you up at eight forty-five, so you be ready."

"Okay. Kurt's going to come with me."

"Fine," Kate said. "Just be sure you're on time."

Once home, Kate got ready for the party. She didn't want to be overdressed; she had always felt that it was much better to be too casual than too formal. But tonight she had no doubts about what she was wearing. It was something that had just come in to the store along with the first shipments of other resort wear, and it had caught Kate's eye from across the selling floor: sapphire-blue silk pants with a matching top, which she would wear with low-heeled snakeskin sandals, gold earrings, and extra-thin gold chains.

She had a quick bite to eat and a drink, and then she was off.

CHAPTER TEN

The discotheque was a bit dingy-looking from the outside; it was, after all, a converted old theater. For a second Kate had a moment of dread: no one would show up; the party would be a bust. But after she gave her card to the man outside the door, and was let inside, her mood lifted immediately.

The room was dazzling—dark with soft, pulsating lighting, music that seemed to be coming from everywhere, the smoky, electric excitement of a good party—and Kate was relieved to see that somehow she had missed that beginning-of-a-party stage that was usually particularly awkward at functions like this. But people had come, and come early. The dance floor—down a ramp from the front door—was fairly empty, filled with people talking rather than dancing. But the bar—along the near wall—was packed, and many of the small tables in the VIP area around the dance floor were filled. Kate recognized dozens of people—models, manufacturers, designers, people who worked at Ivorsen and Shaw—but most of the faces were unfamiliar.

Kate went to the bar and managed to get a drink in the

crush, and then made her way over to one of the small tables, where she spotted Alison.

"This place looks fabulous," Alison said, looking up as Kate sat next to her.

"That wall over there should have the slide show on at any moment," Kate said, pointing to the wall opposite the entrance. "And pretty soon Alexandra and Pierce should be circulating."

"Just walking around, or what?"

"Well, modeling, for one thing. A whole series of outfits we put together—mostly by designers we knew would be here. And handing everyone little cards with different things written on them, like 'Good for one free massage and facial at Ivorsen and Shaw's new beauty and relaxation salon.' Things like that."

"Hey. Sounds great. Drag that girl over here when she comes around."

Kate laughed. "We're not that generous. It all comes out of my paltry ad budget. Alexandra and Pierce are supposed to concentrate on the media people if they can."

"Hell. She doesn't know me. I'll tell her I'm a gossip columnist."

Kate smiled. "Be my guest. But you'll probably fail because if everything is as it has been lately, she won't be taking a step without our dear Kurt."

"Whew. He does turn heads, doesn't he?"

At that moment the music picked up, getting louder and faster. And as Kate looked up, the slide show began. Dramatically spliced pictures of Alexandra and Pierce were flashing in rhythm to the music, and Kate noticed that the spectacle was attracting immediate attention. Kate finished her drink and stood up. "I'm going to circulate and try to find Alexandra, Ally. I'll see you later." She pushed through the now-thick crowd, glancing unobtrusively at everyone's nametag and smiling at people she knew. *Damn,* she thought. For she looked everywhere she could, moving through the crowd and covering the entire floor, and Alexandra was nowhere in sight. Pierce had arrived even before Kate had, and she had spotted him several times already, weaving gracefully through the crowd and smiling his beautiful smile. But Alexandra was another quantity entirely.

At the bar Kate spent five minutes with Jessica Murphy, a woman who had a new fashion-and-beauty call-in show on WZKZ. "The store looks fabulous," Ms. Murphy gushed. "The salon was incredible. Just divine."

Kate smiled. "I'm glad. I'll have to try it myself one of these days."

"My dear, I'd do nothing *else* if I worked in that building every day." She nodded at the wall that was at that moment covered with a shot from the lingerie ad. "Where'd you get the girl?" she demanded. "Just gorgeous."

"Oh, we just . . . found her," Kate said vaguely, not wanting to go into the whole story.

"Tell her rep to give me a call," Ms. Murphy said. "I'd love to have her on sometime."

"I'll do that," Kate said, thinking she *would* do it if Alexandra were anywhere to be found. Where on earth was she? "But if you'll excuse me, I have to find someone," she said, and moved off into the crowd.

She bumped right into Joe Brennan, president of Essences, Limited, a cosmetics company that had been among the most enthusiastic supporters of the Ivorsen and

Shaw revitalization. Essences had just redesigned the packaging on their products, and the change had coincided with the redecoration of I and S's ground floor. Brennan—young, handsome, a maverick in the cosmetics field for years—had turned Essences, Limited, from a faltering concern to one of the country's leading cosmetics companies in less than a year, and Kate had read of his success with great admiration and pleasure. The few times she had met him, she had liked him enormously.

"Kate," he cried, smiling and extending a hand.

"Joe. I'm glad you could come."

"So am I. So are we, actually. Kate, I'd like you to meet my wife, Jennifer Preston Brennan."

"Oh, hello," Kate said, shaking hands with the pretty young woman at Brennan's side. "We've talked on the phone several times," she said. "I hadn't realized you two were married."

"Well, I use my maiden name, Preston, at work," Jennifer said, "since that's what I used before I began working at Essences. By the way, Kate, I looked in at the store yesterday, and I was amazed by the difference. And I love the ads, too. We're going to be doing something similar for the new premium we're marketing—a silk cosmetics purse for every ten-dollar purchase."

"Great," Kate said. "Maybe we can talk about it over lunch next week."

As Kate stayed and talked with Jennifer and Joe for several more minutes, she was intrigued and impressed by their relationship: they worked together, they seemed madly in love, and there was an optimism and contentment that seemed to underlie their whole approach to work and to each other. *This* was what she wished she could have with Ben.

Suddenly there was a commotion down near the entrance. Kate looked across the dance floor, and saw—for a moment only, as the crowd parted—Kurt leading Alexandra down the ramp.

Kate said a quick good-bye to the Brennans and made her way across the dance floor. Through the crowd she could just make the two out: Kurt had Alexandra firmly by the hand, and he was just leading her to one of the few empty VIP tables when Kate caught up to them.

She caught Kurt by the shoulder, and he turned around with a look of surprise that changed instantly to relief—as if, Kate guessed, he was thinking, *Oh, it's only you.*

"What time do you think it is?" Kate yelled. She noticed that Alexandra was now sitting down, apparently uninterested in the event going on around her.

Kurt looked blankly at Kate, saying nothing.

Kate was furious. "Alexandra was supposed to be here at nine o'clock," she blazed. "Before I arrived, and before *anyone* arrived, as a matter of fact. It's now ten o'clock. What the hell happened?"

Kurt smiled lazily. "We're fashionably late," he said.

Kate widened her eyes in anger. "Goddammit, Kurt, Alexandra is a paid model, not some sort of incidental guest. And she's paid to make an appearance—on time—at this party." Kate looked around to see if any attention was being paid to the argument. Luckily, with the crowds, the music, and the models Kate had invited from the Zoli and Ford agencies, no one seemed to be taking any interest in Kate's shouting match with Kurt.

But just as Kate was about to light into Kurt again, she

saw Ben across the room. Her stomach contracted in a knot of tension and she looked quickly away. God, what was going to happen? What approach was she supposed to take? What approach would Ben take?

Against her will she turned again—just to get a glance at him—and she saw he was coming straight toward her. Her heart would have lifted and she would have felt some ray of hope if she hadn't seen the expression on his face. For even at a distance she could see that he was angry. And he looked harried, too, with his dark hair hanging over his forehead and his five o'clock shadow darkly evident.

As Ben approached, Kate searched his eyes for a clue: How did he feel about seeing her? Had anything changed? Did he want to argue, to soothe, to try to patch things up?

But he didn't even look her in the eye.

And when he spoke, it was to Kurt. Not even a hello to Kate. "What's going on?" he demanded.

"She was late," Kate said, more to get Ben to look at her than to answer his question.

But when his gaze met hers, she wished she had said nothing. His eyes were blazing with anger, looking through her rather than at her. "Again? She hasn't done anything but hold people up since she began. What happened? I thought you were sending a car for her."

"I did," Kate said as calmly as she could. "Apparently it was held up. I don't know. Kurt?"

He shrugged. "Sure we kept it waiting. I had to be sure she looked good."

"I've heard *that* before," Kate said, and for a moment Ben looked at her almost thoughtfully.

Then he turned his fury on Kurt. "You. Go somewhere

else. I don't want to see your face."

Kurt's mouth dropped open. "You can't—"

"I can do whatever the hell I want," Ben warned.

He turned to Kate. "Kate. You get this little dream-girl into gear. If we're lucky no one will have noticed anything wrong."

And he stormed off into the crowd without giving Kate another glance.

Kate could hardly believe it; he hadn't even said hello. He wouldn't even have spoken to her if he hadn't seen her arguing with Kurt. And she realized, as she tried to blink back tears and watch Kurt head for the exit, that in the back of her mind, she had been expecting Ben to make everything right tonight. And it hadn't happened that way.

He could have tried to convince her to come to California after all; he could have said he was sorry for walking out. But he had obviously taken deep offense at what she had said, and he wanted to be away from her.

And now, as she recalled the look of cold hostility in Ben's eyes, she realized there was a very, very good possibility that Ben didn't just want to be away from her for a few days: there was a chance he wanted to be away from her forever.

Kate went up to the bar and got herself another Scotch and soda; she had a long night to get through, and she couldn't break down in tears in the middle of the party. She would have to bear up and forget about Ben for now—put him and his eyes and his cold, hard voice out of her mind for the moment.

And somehow she managed. She instructed Alexandra to pull herself together and start circulating. She then forced herself to talk to people she knew and people she didn't know, forced herself to smile and listen carefully and laugh and joke and make small talk. And, except for Kate's inner turmoil, the evening went smoothly.

Oscar Ivorsen, president of Ivorsen and Shaw, gave a short, impassioned speech that shocked Kate with its sincerity, optimism, and enthusiasm. At the store Ivorsen was a figurehead more than anything else, a brass nameplate on the door of an office that was usually empty, its occupant on the golf courses of Westchester and Connecticut. But the speech was actually inspiring, and the generous round of applause afterward showed that others had been caught up in Ivorsen's enthusiasm as well. And in terms of morale and the confidence of manufacturers and consignment outfits, the speech was priceless.

The food was excellent, too. Kate got dozens of compliments on the party from guests of all kinds, and she conducted six or seven good, solid interviews with representatives of the media. It was a glittering night of success.

But Ben seemed to be gone.

Kate couldn't be certain. There were over three hundred people there, crammed on to the dance floor, spilling over the banquettes, packed six deep at the bar. But she knew, instinctively, that he was gone.

At one point Kate saw Tommy Sullivan, Ben's art assistant. He was drunk and almost hysterically happy, and when Kate asked him if he had seen Ben, he shrugged wildly, slapping a woman standing next to him in his drunken gesture. Kate smiled and moved on.

Pierce was doing admirably, moving gracefully through the crowd with his gold mail pouch full of cards. He had relaxed as time had gone on and the guests had had more to drink, and he was now talking and joking with many—especially the women—as he handed them their cards.

Kate made her way up to him and took him by the elbow. "You're fantastic," she whispered in his ear. "Just great. Keep it up and you'll be the star of the evening."

He smiled, but grew quickly serious. "What happened to Alexandra?" he leaned down and asked. "Is she all right?"

"She's fine," Kate yelled. "Kurt just got her here late, that's all—for no reason other than that he wanted her to 'look good.' "

Pierce shook his head. "Bastard. But it's her own fault. Kurt doesn't chain her to his side. You've got to learn to take care of yourself in this business or you'll be eaten alive."

Kate nodded. "You're probably right. And keep up the good work, Pierce. You're dazzling the ladies."

"That's what I'm here for," he said, and smiled, waved a lithe hand, and moved off again into the crowd.

Finally, the evening began to wind down. Alexandra and Pierce were still going strong, charming all with whom they spoke, intriguing those they missed. But Kate surveyed the crowd and saw that most of the more important guests had left, and she decided it was finally time to leave. The music was too loud to talk above anyway, so Kate went downstairs and got her coat, and went out into the cold night air for a taxi.

And then, once in the cab, she let her feelings come to the surface. And she was suddenly dizzy, almost ill with confusion, sick from the stale smell of smoke that had suffused her clothes at the party.

The party. She had worried about it, made it a focus of her life for the past few weeks; it had turned out very well, exceeding her most optimistic hopes; and she hardly cared.

For Ben was apparently content to break off communications completely, to leave things as they had been when he had walked out of Kate's apartment.

At the party he hadn't even looked into her eyes with anything except utter coldness; he had barely looked at her at all.

And Kate was suddenly swamped with regrets: What if she hadn't ever spoken up? What if she could have taken back her words?

But that would have only postponed the inevitable. For she would still be who she was; he would still be who he was; and nothing would have changed. Yet she hadn't meant what she had said to be a good-bye. . . .

The next morning Kate awakened with a vague hangover—aching, fuzzy, slightly dizzy. For a brief moment—a blessed moment—she thought her encounter last night with Ben had been a dream.

But with an unwished-for clarity she remembered the whole scene in a painful vision. And by the gray, drizzly light of the morning there was an inexplicable but definite feeling of finality to the memory. Last night the experience had seemed dreamlike, indefinite, from music that was too loud and drinks that were too strong; but now, it was all too clear.

Kate got ready for work clumsily and inefficiently, her body grudgingly going through the motions of the morning routine: shower, get dressed, put on makeup, drag yourself out the door.

At the store everyone looked a bit drained and pale, just a little the worse for wear than yesterday. As Kate rode up in the crowded elevator, she accepted congratulations for the evening with a forced smile, and shut herself in her office with a cup of black coffee and the *Times.*

Mechanically, she turned to the page on which fashion and society news appeared. And her heart skipped a beat as she began to read: "Last night bright lights of Seventh Avenue gathered to celebrate the launching of Ivorsen and Shaw's new and ambitious ad campaign. It was a glorious party celebrating a glorious store whose reputation has unjustly faded over the years. As one woman was heard remarking to another, 'The whole store is *divine.*' And indeed, judging by the swarm of fans there to celebrate, the world will soon be beating a path to those East Fifty-second Street doors once again."

Kate smiled. Lovely. She couldn't have asked for a more positive article. She picked up the phone, buzzed Linda, and asked her to be sure all board members received copies of the article by the afternoon with a memo she'd give her in a few minutes.

She hung up, and then, hand still on the receiver, hesitated. It would have been so natural to call Ben if this had been only a few short days ago—to share in the excitement, share the pleasure, enjoy a joint triumph. But now everything was different.

She went back to her work, composing a memo to the board that was positive without being overly self-congratulatory. The message had to be clear: Yes, gentlemen, parties like this do work, and our ad dollars were well spent. It would have been a simple memo to write—just a line or two—if her mind had been clear.

But now—now the task seemed Herculean.

She wished she could talk to Ben, wished she could turn back the clock and make all that had happened disappear.

She sighed, staring at the newspaper. And suddenly she realized she hadn't even given any thought to the future of the campaign: how would she and Ben work together from now on? Would she be able to look him in the eye knowing the warmth she loved was gone? Would she be able to pretend she wasn't being torn apart inside as she listened to that voice she adored?

She closed her eyes, trying to think. What would she do?

And then she knew she would have to go on as well as she could, just as she had done last night. She would have to ignore and hide and suppress her feelings, and go on.

And perhaps now was the best time to start. For she wanted to tell Ben—the one she loved, not the "new" Ben—about the clipping; she wanted to try to share some of the triumph; and it would be among the easiest topics they would ever discuss again.

She dialed Blake-Canfield, gave her name and asked for Ben, and then tried to slow the beating of her heart as she waited for Ben to come on.

She heard a click, then "Kate," in a voice that was completely neutral, chilling, devoid of clues.

"Uh, hi," she said. Suddenly she was swept with fear: *why* had she called? It was too soon after last night. "I, uh, thought I'd let you know about the *Times.*"

There was a pause, just a beat. Then: "Yes, I saw it," he answered in the same unreadable tone.

She waited for him to say more. But there was no reply.

"Well," she muttered, "I guess that's about it." She

closed her eyes. God, why had she said that?

"By the way," Ben said, "you'll be working with a woman named Christina Casey for a while, Kate. I've decided to stay on in California for an extra three weeks—we have some business out there and I'm combining my time off with that." He paused. "I'll be staying at the Drake," he said, and gave her the address and phone number. "I don't know if—" He hesitated. "Well, there it is if you need it."

"Okay," she said, her throat closing over her voice.

"Well. I guess that about wraps it up," he said. "I'll be here the rest of the afternoon, and then I'm off."

"Right," she said quietly. "Good-bye."

She put the phone down and put her head in her hands. Now there was no question. It was definitely over. Ben was fleeing, putting as much distance between them as he could—and for as long as he could. Kate had spoken her mind; she had told him she wasn't happy, that she didn't want to go out west with him; and her words had been enough to make him end it completely. And it had ended as inevitably as all her other relationships had ended.

Kate closed her eyes. *Except Ben was different,* she said to herself. *God, how I loved him.*

Yet she knew that this time, there was no way out—no way back in. This was no misunderstanding, no tragic error that could be reversed at the last minute. For no matter how much she wanted to believe otherwise, Kate knew there was no solution this time. She had stood up for herself, rescuing herself at a very steep price from the most important relationship of her life. Yet if she hadn't done what she had done, it would have cost her—once again—her self. For no matter how she resolved the minor questions, there would always remain a sobering and immutable fact: if Ben couldn't accept her as she was, she would be playing a role for him, perhaps for the rest of her life. And Ben obviously couldn't accept her for herself; he couldn't even accept the fact that she wanted to be true to herself. And so it was over forever.

Kate sipped at her now cold coffee and looked at the mass of papers on her desk. Insertion orders from newspapers; magazines that didn't interest her a bit; a stack of interoffice memos—most completely without importance—that seemed a mile high.

At least she was good enough to do her job mechanically for a while, even if her heart wasn't in it. And she began to move through her work and through the morning slowly and surely, half her mind on the job and half on Ben. And gradually a new anger was born, a feeling much closer to what she had felt the other night. She may have been the one who had started the argument, but he hadn't even been able to fight. He had walked out, washing his hands of the matter as if it didn't exist. And it was over because of *his* stubbornness, his refusal to let her think and act and even feel as she wanted. He was the one who had no faith in her, who wanted to be analyst rather than lover, critic rather than partner. And she had made a choice she had never been able to make before: she had chosen to be honest with herself over all else.

Just before lunch Linda came in with some papers for Kate to sign. "Oh, you look awful," she said.

Kate managed a wan smile. "Yes, well, I'm a little hung-over."

"Do you want me to take over so you can go home? And

what about the in-stores? Aren't Alexandra and Pierce supposed to do one tomorrow?"

"Yes. I have to call Alexandra. God knows what kind of shape she's in. And thanks, but I'll manage."

"Good luck," Linda said. "Let me know if you need anything." And she left the office and shut the door.

Kate dreaded calling Alexandra. She would have to lay down the law for her, and she wasn't completely certain of the best approach; for she didn't know how much of Alexandra's misbehavior and lateness stemmed from Kurt's destructive influence. She sighed. Perhaps Alexandra was simply a hopeless case, one of those talented, star-quality newcomers who every year and in every field fall under the influence of someone bent on destroying them. Perhaps she didn't have a chance as long as she was involved with Kurt. But perhaps she did. Kate simply didn't know how to make the judgment.

But the first step, in any case, was to talk to her.

Kate had to let the phone ring six times, and then Kurt answered. At first it was difficult to get Kurt even to hand the phone over to Alexandra. But when he finally did, Alexandra made Kate's decision even more difficult; for she was wildly apologetic, nearly in tears and quite concerned over how much she had inconvenienced Kate and the campaign. And she promised with apparently deep sincerity that she would be on her best behavior from now on.

The next day, however, as Kate waited with Pierce for Alexandra in "The Sporting Life," I and S's sporting-goods department, her doubts bloomed anew. The two models were scheduled to demonstrate exercise equipment from twelve o'clock to one, and Kate had told Alexandra to be there at eleven, thinking that even if she were a bit late, it still wouldn't interfere with the demonstration. But it was now eleven forty-five; Kate had called Alexandra's and Kurt's apartments several times over the past hour; and Alexandra was nowhere to be found.

Kate looked at Pierce, calm and serene as usual as he lounged on a weight-lifting bench. "This is going to be a wonderful promotion," Kate said sarcastically. "Most of the equipment we planned to demonstrate is pretty much geared to women. And no offense, Pierce, but two models are more than twice as good as one."

He smiled and looked at his watch. "Don't worry, Kate. I'll handle it if I have to. Do you want me to change?"

"Oh, you can wait a bit," she said. She looked at Pierce carefully. "What do you think of Alexandra, by the way? You must know her better than any of us by now."

He shook his head, his handsome pale blue eyes placid as he said, "I really hardly know her. Kurt keeps her on a very tight emotional rein." He shrugged. "I've seen it happen dozens of times, though—in acting, mostly. Maybe she'll get out from under his control. But if she does, she'll just go looking for another one."

"Mm," Kate said, thinking for a moment about herself. Surely she had been only a pale version of Alexandra when she had been with Kurt. He had dominated her in only a very few areas. But what Pierce had said was disturbing nevertheless. For she didn't like to think she resembled Alexandra in any way; and she knew that, in the past, she had.

And the heartbreak of it was that she had had to break away from a man she truly did love in order to save herself from repeating the pattern.

Kate tried to bring her thoughts back to the promotion. She looked at her watch: ten to twelve. People were starting to come to the area, glancing at the TWELVE O'CLOCK DEMONSTRATION sign and moving on a bit. They were waiting, Kate recognized, interested in the demonstration but unwilling to waste time waiting for something when there was a whole store to look at. And if the demonstration didn't begin soon, they would leave, either drifting away without giving it much thought or stalking off in annoyance.

And then, just as Kate was about to go over and talk with Gloria Lennox, the woman who was going to narrate the demonstration, Alexandra came running in—alone.

"I'm sorry," she said breathlessly. "Really sorry. I'll explain later. Where do I change?"

"Go in there," Kate said, pointing to the women's try-on room. "Your things are at the front. And, Pierce, you know where to go."

"Right," he said, saluting.

Kate stayed at the exercise area with Gloria Lennox and the salespeople, and a few minutes later Alexandra and Pierce came racing out of their changing areas, both looking appropriately young and fit and attractive in their very expensive maroon workout clothes.

And the promotion began. The newest best-selling exercise record—music only, with an accompanying aerobics booklet—began pulling customers in with its quiet but steady rhythm, and Gloria Lennox began her talk as Alexandra and Pierce warmed up to the beat.

People came, drifting in from the Trattoria down the floor, "Best Toys for Best Kids" in the other direction, from "Active Swimwear" across the hall. And as Alexandra and Pierce worked together and apart, demonstrating the newest in weight-training for women, aerobics for men, and tandem exercises for both, the crowd grew. It was made up of both men and women—some interested in the equipment, most interested in Alexandra or Pierce, all certain at some level to be inspired by their youth and energy.

Kate noticed a familiar-looking man in the crowd; she was certain she had seen him somewhere recently, but she couldn't place him. And then her attention shifted back to Alexandra. She was eyeing a man in the crowd—handsome, gray-haired, obviously wealthy—with a look of such frank sexuality that even in a promotion such as the rather physical one going on, it was out of place. She was supposed to be spotting for Pierce as he demonstrated the weight-lifting bench and its properties, but she had eyes only for this man. And then, as suddenly as the flirting had begun, it shifted. Alexandra had a new target—this one younger, very casually dressed, at the front of the crowd. He smiled at her, and she shifted again as the exercise ended for a moment and Pierce moved the weights back to the edge of the demonstration area. Alexandra had a peculiar gleam in her eye as she picked up two three-kilo weights and brought them to the edge of the crowd.

"These are specially designed to be handled easily," she said in a soft, seductive voice. "And even if you're the strongest of men," she said breathily, her eyes roving the crowd, "they can make you strong in places you never even thought to exercise." She walked up to a man across from where Kate stood, at the edge of the crowd. He was in his late thirties, tall, fair, classically handsome, dressed in a beautifully tailored suit. "How would you like to try?"

she cooed, coming up so close to the man that she was nearly touching him.

At first he was a bit taken aback by having been singled out this way. But then the light of surprise in his eyes turned to one of interest as he smiled. "Anything to please a beautiful young woman," he said, taking the weights from her hands. "Now, just what did you have in mind?"

Alexandra turned crimson, as if she had been sleepwalking and just awakened in the middle of some embarrassing act. "I, uh, they're very light," she stammered, and a ripple of laughter swept through the crowd.

Kate was completely puzzled. What on earth had Alexandra just been up to?

The rest of the demonstration was uneventful in terms of Alexandra; and in terms of sales, it was excellent. People bought weights, books, exercise mats, workout suits, virtually everything the department stocked.

And so the promotion had been a hit, even if parts had been a bit mysterious.

Later on, after Alexandra and Pierce had changed and Pierce had gone off for the afternoon, Kate took Alexandra to Il Trattoria for a talk.

After they were seated and had ordered, Kate looked at Alexandra carefully. "I want you to understand," she began slowly, "that I'm talking to you both as an employer and as a friend. Both are important. You obviously know, Alexandra, that we aren't going to be able to keep you on if you keep being late and not quite right for the in-person promotions."

"I have a contract," she said in the naturally small voice she used when not in public.

Kate shook her head. "Your contract demands a lot of

things, Alexandra, and one of them is that you be on time."

"But my uncle—"

"Listen to me," Kate said gently but firmly. "I'm not going to argue because it's not worth arguing about. There's nothing *to* argue about. Alexandra, I don't have to tell you that what you've been doing lately would be completely unacceptable to anyone who hired you. If you want to get ahead, you're going to have to make a lot of changes. It has nothing to do with me, it's just a fact. What I don't understand is why you're doing what you're doing. Why are you late when you could be on time? Isn't it important for you to do well?"

Alexandra was looking down into her lap. When she raised her head, her eyes were brimming with tears. "It's more important than anything. And it's more important to Kurt than anything."

"Forget about Kurt for a minute, Alexandra, and—"

"Why?" she demanded. "Just because you might be jealous or—"

"I'm not jealous," Kate said calmly.

Alexandra looked skeptical. "Well, I don't want to forget about him even for a minute. He has everything to do with my success."

"Then why are you on the brink of getting fired?"

"You wouldn't do that. My uncle—"

"Your uncle," Kate interrupted, "isn't so hot on this campaign himself. He wants you in it, but he's not going to want you in it any more than I will if you keep showing up cranky and late. And what was that all about today, anyway?"

Alexandra flushed. "Kurt thought it would be a good

idea." She sighed. "I didn't. We had a really big fight and that's why I was late. But when I came I decided he was probably right. He told me to make a big splash, and I did."

Kate sighed and shook her head. "Don't you understand? He's pushing you in directions that aren't even right. He pushes you so hard that you're a nervous wreck. Then he tells you something that isn't even valid."

Alexandra raised her chin. "*You* don't know. He's getting me into the papers. I'm going to be a personality in my own right. There was a man from the gossip column of the *Post* there today, even. Kurt called him and he came."

The *Post.* So that was where Kate had seen the man at the demonstration; he had been at Xenon the other night. "Kurt had no right to do that," Kate said, looking intently at Alexandra. "And what was the exact purpose, anyway?"

"I told you," Alexandra said. "Maybe you don't know that certain models get written about all the time. They're not just in ads."

Kate sighed. Alexandra was so naive she was almost impossible to deal with. Clearly it would be impossible to make her see the light; all she could do was convince her to shape up for the campaign.

And finally, by the end of lunch, she had extracted a grudging promise from Alexandra that she would clear all "plans" of Kurt's, and that she wouldn't be late for any more of the promotions. On this there was not even a gray area; if she was late, she would be fired.

The next day Alexandra was on time—without Kurt—when she arrived for a promotion in the men's wear department with Pierce. But almost as soon as the session began, she was up to yesterday's tricks, flirting with the men in the audience and again approaching them. At first Kate was furious. She had talked with Alexandra only yesterday! But interest took the place of annoyance as she saw the effect of Alexandra's moves. She was more confident today, much more sure of herself, and her performance worked where it hadn't the day before. She was less a young girl's misguided interpretation of a siren, more an attractive young woman as she helped one man on with a tie, seductively helped another on with a vest. She talked to the women, too, charming a few, and then Pierce joined in in an obvious approving and good-humored manner. And as Kate put the fact that the whole scheme was Kurt's idea out of her mind, she saw that it was in fact a beautiful addition to the campaign. They had been featuring the Ivorsen and Shaw couple in ads. Why not let people get to know them in the store? If people came to see them, there was absolutely nothing wrong with letting them talk.

She almost laughed at the idea's simplicity. And she watched the rest of the session in relaxed enjoyment.

That afternoon the success of Kurt's plan was obvious in another corner as well. When Kate returned to her office, Linda rushed in after her, waving a copy of the New York *Post.* "You're not going to believe this!" she cried. "Turn to page six."

Kate opened to page six of the tabloid—one of the three or more daily gossip pages the paper usually carried. And there, in the middle of the page, was a glowing account of the audience-participation demonstration.

"This is fantastic," Kate said. "I don't believe it!"

But there was more. Most of the major dailies and fashion newspapers contained similar articles to the *Post* 's, insuring that I and S had truly reestablished itself in the fashion world.

Kate left the store that day smiling, wondering at the fact that the promotion was exceeding her most optimistic hopes. There was a cloud of disappointment at the thought that Ben wasn't there to share her news. But she had developed a self-protective shell of skepticism over the past couple of days, and she looked at Ben's absence as something she could and should have expected. He was like the others; just more subtle in his faults.

Yet, at certain moments—at night as she lay in bed, recalling his feverish touch, in the morning right after dreams—she was more vulnerable, less guarded against her old feelings. And at those times she missed him deeply, remembering the Ben she loved.

Irrationally, she blamed him for having left her behind, resented him for not having been trustworthy; he had run off as all the others always had in their own ways, if only emotionally. And when part of her protested and said, *You drove him away; he asked you to go with him,* it meant little. He had obviously decided that she was right, and had gone off in search of another, more perfect, love.

On Thursday, Kate rented a car and drove up to her mother's in the morning, dread extending to her fingertips from the pit of her stomach. She was not ready for the unspoken questions, the raised brow over arriving alone, the veiled comments about the pleasures of marriage. And she knew that after the meal, when she and her mother would be washing dishes together in the kitchen, the unspoken questions would finally be asked. Kate would try to answer calmly, explaining that yes, she still wanted to get married if she found the right man; no, obviously she hadn't; and no, she wasn't still seeing the man she had mentioned. It was not going to be the best of days.

And the day turned out exactly as Kate had expected: her mother's new husband was much like the second—paunchy, gruff, uncommunicative; her mother was in a state of hectic, forced happiness that nearly brought tears to Kate's eyes; and Kate lied just to be kind, telling her mother when they were alone together that she liked her new husband.

When Kate arrived back at her apartment, she was in a black mood—depressed by the visit to her mother's, weighted down from too much eating and drinking. Yet she felt she would never fall asleep: too many thoughts were jangling through her head, too many memories of Ben kept coming through. She remembered how he had once said he would spend Thanksgiving alone, before he had decided to go to California, and how her heart had pulled at the thought. Now he was three thousand miles away—perhaps with Celia and the kids, perhaps alone, perhaps with someone new. And there *would* be someone new, she was certain. A perfect love, if he could ever find one.

She padded to the kitchen and took out an opened bottle of wine that had been chilling in the refrigerator, and brought the bottle and a glass out to the living room. Maybe it would relax her—that and a little music—and she turned on a quiet classical music station and settled onto the couch.

Yes, she could just imagine Ben in California: telling

some new woman about his first marriage, about how he was so "ready" to try again. But he wasn't ready; he distanced himself as surely as someone like Kurt; the only difference was in the intensity and method. And the fact that he didn't see the problem himself. For every time he found fault with Kate, he distanced her; every time he tried to make her into someone she was not, he drove her away; and every time he told her she wasn't ready for love, he destroyed the love they had.

But he didn't see that; no, he didn't see that at all. Out there in California, he was probably—if he was thinking of her at all—remembering her with regret, wishing she had been "different" so things could have worked out between them. And he was fooling himself.

And suddenly, consumed with anger, Kate didn't want to see him again, didn't want to look into those beautiful golden eyes and see only neutrality reflected back. She had seen love in those eyes; she didn't want to see that that love had gone. And she didn't want to hear that wonderful voice devoid of affection, telling her in a monotone some fact about the campaign she didn't even want to hear.

Kate wanted it over, clean and simple. And more than anything, she wanted him to see what had gone wrong, to see things were *not* what he had thought. And she wanted him to take some of the responsibility for their failure.

Kate opened the drawer of the end table next to the couch and took out her stationery. She'd write to him; she'd write everything she felt, everything she wanted to say to him, and it would be over for good.

She drank more wine, started the letter six times, angrily turned off the radio so she could concentrate. And finally the words began to flow:

Dear Ben:

I know that letters like this are usually regretted, never forgotten, never welcome. I know I could call; I know you expect to talk to me, to see me when you get back—which is why I'm writing this letter.

Ben, I don't want to see you when you come back. That's very painful for me to write. Part of me doesn't even mean it. But I'm writing it because it's what I want and what I know is right.

I don't think you know what happened between us. When we last spoke and you said we'd talk when you got back, I think you thought all the problems would have somehow disappeared by then. But they're not going to, Ben. And I don't want to pick up where we left off, hard as that is for me to face.

When you said I was always drawn to men who run off, you were right; I've always known that, and I've told you that. What you didn't see is that you were another of those men, in your own way. I didn't see it at first. All your talk of being 'ready,' of looking for a woman to share your life with, was very seductive, and I thought you were different, that you were that rare man who really does mean those things.

You told me you didn't think I was ready for love, that I wasn't ready to trust. I don't think *you're* ready for love. You've driven me away at every opportunity, drawing me back with words of love and promises of sincerity. But each time you've distanced me again.

I have to protect myself. You were different in that I stood up to you in ways I had never stood up to any man before. I'm learning—finally—to speak out for myself. And if I went back to you, I'd lose myself all over again.

We came close. What we had was the best thing I've ever had. But it can never be again—you'll always be looking for your perfect woman, Ben, and I'm not going to change.

I don't want to see you when you get back. I know I could if I had to, so if it's impossible for you to hand the account over to Christina Casey, I'll understand. But please try.

I love you.
Kate

She didn't reread the letter. Deep inside she felt that what she had written was right, that she'd never be able to write it again in a million years if she had to. And if it was right, it had to be mailed before she changed her mind.

It was the only way: it would be cleaner this way, like a deep wound made with the sharpest of knives.

And she sealed it, stamped it, padded out to the hallway, and dropped it down the chute.

When she finally went to bed, she fell into a deep, dreamless sleep, completely exhausted.

When Kate awakened the next morning, her first thought was of the letter: the memory of writing it had lodged in her brain like a stone, and it brought with it pain but no regret, a kind of sickening dread along with a certainty it had been the right thing to do. And it *had* made her feel better: she had performed a final act, and the world—and her life—could now go on.

That small part of the world that I and S occupied was in chaos that morning when Kate arrived, just as the doors were opening. She had never seen such a crowd at the store. And while today—the day after Thanksgiving—was traditionally the biggest shopping day of the year, the crowd was impressive even so.

As Kate made her way inside, she spotted Andrew Smithfield, of the I and S board, coming in the door next to hers. "Good morning," she called out.

He smiled. "Beautiful, isn't it? And I'm willing to say I was wrong, Miss Churchill. The campaign is a beaut."

The day was magnificent in terms of sales and morale, and Kate was caught up in her job again for the first time since she and Ben had had the fight. *New York* magazine was going to run an item about I and S in its "Intelligencer" column, and a crew from Eyewitness News was coming to film the Friday-night shopping crush later on, for a story on the start of the Christmas shopping season.

At the end of the day Linda, eyes shining brightly, came in to Kate's office. "Guess what?"

Kate smiled. "What?"

"Kurt Reeves has just been fired. I just heard."

"Well, isn't that interesting," she said musingly. And though she hated being pleased over someone else's misfortune, she couldn't help smiling just a bit. He had made her life difficult in hundreds of ways over the past months. And she had to admit she would be glad to have him gone, or at least as far away as possible. Of course, if she knew Alexandra, chances were Kurt would still be very much around; but at least he couldn't interfere in any official capacity.

* * *

Kate had an excellent weekend, thinking about Ben only when she slowed down. She went shopping, actually getting caught up in some of the Christmas spirit that seemed to be everywhere, and she had dinner with Alison, which was always fun.

The letter had helped more than she had anticipated; it was as if, once having set her feelings to paper, Kate was free of them, and she felt much lighter and more clear-headed than she had felt in ages.

When Kate returned to her office Monday morning, Christina Casey called and set up a meeting to discuss an expansion of the campaign.

As Kate hung up, it was a bittersweet moment. The campaign had been such a success; and Ben had been the catalyst of the campaign. It had all come out better than anyone had dreamed. But the man who had begun it all, changing Kate's life in the process, was forever gone. And just as Kate had begun to allow herself to dream—of fulfillment, true happiness, true satisfaction—the dream had been torn from her grasp.

At the end of the day Kate sat alone in her office, the sky dark behind her, horns honking in the street below. There was a store filled with people right below her, but she felt utterly alone, isolated, a million miles away from the rest of the world.

And she *was* alone. No one knew or cared where she was at that moment. They were shopping, laughing, talking, planning. . . .

"Kate."

She looked up, her heart in a vise.

Ben was standing in the doorway, beautiful hazel eyes

shining into hers. "Kate," he murmured, coming in, reaching out for her with both arms.

She turned away, horrified by the sea of emotions she was nearly drowning in. God! She hadn't known how painful it would be to look into those eyes. She had dreaded seeing neutrality. But what she saw now was love.

"We have to talk," he said.

She turned her eyes upon his. "The reason I wrote to you," she said, trying to control her voice, "was so that this wouldn't happen."

His eyes shone with emotion. "Don't do this," he said quietly.

"Don't do what?" she blazed. "You come in here, Ben, after I write asking you *not* to, and then you tell me not to do this. What happened to your trip?"

"I came back as soon as I got your letter," he said quietly. "Kate. Come. Please. At least sit down with me."

She rose, knowing it was the path of least resistance. As she walked with him the short distance to the couch, he put a hand on her shoulder, and she almost cried over the memory of his touch.

She tried to gather strength. When they had seated themselves, she turned to him with narrowed eyes. "Why are you here?" she demanded.

"Because I love you," he said quietly. "And I'm not giving you up."

She laughed incredulously. "You're not—? What about me? Or shouldn't I trust my feelings? I forgot—I have such poor judgment, according to you."

He closed his eyes and shook his head. When he opened them, his eyes were shining with emotion. "Dammit, Kate, what happened? I tried to understand; I really tried.

When I left, I thought I was giving myself time to think—and giving you time to think as well. It wasn't the end—not then. What happened? Why the letter?"

"I saw that it was impossible," she said, her voice strong. "You didn't even see what the problem was, Ben. You didn't even see that it was impossible, that it had to be over at some point—"

"But it wasn't over, Kate—it was never over for me."

She looked at him skeptically. "What about when you walked out of my apartment without a word, when you hardly looked at me at the party, when you were as cold as ice over the phone the next day?"

"I didn't know what you wanted," he said quietly. "You were obviously very angry, Kate. You were the one who didn't want to go to California—remember that. I wanted to give you room. And at the time I almost hated you—for ruining what had been the best relationship of my life. I really did want nothing to do with you for a while. But I didn't want that to be forever."

She sighed. "You could have said something," she said. "You could have told me how you felt." She shook her head. "But it doesn't matter anyway. Don't you see? There's no chance for us. You've never even seen that you're constantly driving me away. And I'm tired of that. I don't need it. And I don't want to fall into the trap again." She sighed. "Maybe that's why I fell"—it was too late to stop—"fell in love with you," she said quietly. "Because I knew you didn't *really* want me. You were like all the others—safe, unattainable, predictable. But I'm different now. I want a man who really, truly loves me."

"Kate," he said quietly, "you *were* right. I was afraid and I didn't even know it. But that's over. I love you and want you and need you as deeply as any one human being can."

She looked into his clear amber eyes, fighting the emotions at war inside. *Oh, God,* she thought. *I love him so much, I hadn't known it would be this difficult.*

"Kate, do you love me?" he asked quietly.

Tears brimmed in her eyes as she nodded, her voice gone to emotion.

He took her in his arms then, and she fell to him with an ease born of deep hunger, deep need, deep love. The feeling of his warm strong arms around her, his familiar scent as she buried her face into his shoulders, the memories that came rushing back, were all too much for her. How could she ever separate from him? They were one—they had been one in the deepest of ways—and she needed him.

He rested his head against hers, and they held each other. "Kate," he whispered. "I'm so glad."

Tears came as she remembered another time he had said those words, when they had first made love—the night she had realized how much she loved him.

And then part of her began to pull away again, charged with fear and questions: what would happen next? What *could* happen next? What had happened to her resolves? She fought with herself—part of her loving this feeling of being in his arms more than anything in the world, part protesting it couldn't last.

Finally, she raised her head and looked into his eyes. "Maybe love can't do it," she said. "It didn't work before, Ben."

He shook his head slowly, his eyes deep and clear. "Because I was holding back," he said quietly. "Just as you said. And you were holding back, just as I said, Kate. But now—now it's different."

"But for how long?" she asked. "I just can't—it hurt enough before, Ben. Later, when it's been deeper—"

"I want you forever," he said softly, gazing into her eyes. "Forever, Kate, as my wife."

"Oh, Ben," she said, laughing and crying at the same time. "It's such a beautiful thought." To have him always, to give herself over to the love she had been fighting and fearing and wanting. . . .

"Say yes, Kate."

She smiled, running her fingers through the softness of his hair. "I don't—I just don't know."

"I promise you something, Kate," he said quietly. "You were right about my search for the perfect woman. I had found her and I was afraid. That woman is you, Kate. It took your good-bye to make me see that. There *is* such a thing as perfection, Kate, when you love another as I love you, as I love everything about you."

"I love you so much," she murmured.

And she wrapped her arms around him and kissed him in a long, deep kiss, a perfect kiss that sealed their love forever.

She was a
prima ballerina–
torn between two men
and her passion to dance
Encore
BY MONIQUE RAPHEL HIGH
author of the bestselling The Four Winds of Heaven
"A huge, colorful novel. A strong blend of
passion, tragedy and art set against
the exotic and exciting world of
dance."—Publishers Weekly
A Dell Book $3.95 12363-1